# honeybites

### I. S. Belle

Kindle eBook ASIN: B0CTC148SN

IngramSpark Print ISBN: 978-1-067-01410-0

KDP Paperback ISBN: 979-8-324-13936-0

# content warnings

Violence, murder, gore, bullying, nonconsensual blood drinking, underage drinking, animal death, addiction, and once again, a surprising amount of vomit.

*"Hell is a teenage girl."*

—— *Needy Lesnicky*

chapter
**one**

SADIE GREER WOKE UP DEAD.

White tiles gleamed overhead. Smooth porcelain curved against her back. She was propped up in a bathtub, smeared with dirt.

Sadie frowned up at the familiar ceiling tiles. She hadn't been in this bathroom in *years*. They still had the Spice Girls mug holding the toothbrushes; bright pink bath bombs in a vase on the sink.

Honey Williams leaned into view, her strawberry blonde hair matted with filth.

"Took your time," she said. "I had to knock you out, sorry not sorry. You kept trying to eat that birdwatcher."

"What the hell are you talking about?" Sadie tried to say. What came out was: "*Whhhyalboo?*"

Honey laughed. It sounded strained. A splatter of red blood highlighted her defined cheekbone.

Sadie's stomach howled. She lurched up, smearing her open mouth against Honey's cheek—

—only to be pushed back into the bathtub, Honey's grip a vice around her shoulder.

"Calm *down*, snacky bitch. Didn't you get enough?"

Sadie blinked. Her head throbbed, a strange patch of numbness clustering at the back of her skull. Memories started to trickle back from the last few bizarre weeks: burying a body. Agreeing to go on a road trip with her ex-best friend to murder the indie band who turned her into a vampire. All those grimy motel bathrooms. The disastrous last confrontation with the indie band when Honey's sire escaped and Honey had to turn Sadie into a vampire before she bled out.

Then the long drive back home for senior year. Stopping at the side of the road to chase down a cow and drink it dry. Finally arriving in their hometown, Sadie unable to think about anything that wasn't the ravenous roaring hunger for more.

*Just a few deer*, Honey had said as they cruised into town in Sadie's van. *Then I'm heading home and taking a shower. I don't care if we don't sweat anymore, I still feel gross.*

Parking on the edge of town. Slinking through the woods. Chasing down a deer, then two, their throats opening so tenderly under Sadie's fangs.

The memories blurred. Sadie remembered crouching, drinking, fur against her lips. Then a low gasp. Sadie had whipped around and seen—

She squeezed her eyes shut. "Did I...was that your ex-boyfriend's *dad*?"

"Mr. Lu, looking for owls," Honey confirmed. "What a *nerd*."

She rubbed Sadie's brow with a washcloth. It came away smudged with black blood. Sadie frowned again, another memory sliding into place:

Lunging. Mr. Lu screaming, the sound dim compared to the sweet noise of his shoulder ripping under her teeth. A pair of arms around her, yanking her back. Fighting back, trying to get back to the man's bleeding shoulder, snarling and straining until finally a sharp pain exploded in her head and everything faded.

"You knocked me out," Sadie mumbled, tongue thick.

"Uh-huh. Actually I, um..." Honey grimaced. "I kinda caved your head in with a rock?"

"You *what*?" Sadie lifted her hand toward the numb spot at the back of her head.

Honey caught it. "Everything's *totally* fine," she said, smiling like she did when she wanted a guy to focus on how hot she was and not how badly she messed up. "Hats are in fashion right now."

She rubbed a thumb over Sadie's hand. Sadie stared. Both their nails were crusted with black blood. Their wrists, too. Honey's crop top was drenched with it.

"You *caved my head in*?"

"Well, you wouldn't go down!" Honey threw Sadie's limp hand back onto Sadie's lap and picked up the flannel again. "*Excuse* me for not letting you murder Mr. Lu because he was stupid enough to go birdwatching at the worst time ever. Who goes into the woods at night, *alone*? Moron. He was *asking* to get murdered."

She rubbed the flannel over Sadie's face, scraping dirt and dead leaves.

Sadie swallowed. "But he's not murdered, right? He's alive?"

"What? Yeah, he's fine. Summer's already messaging me about her dad being in hospital. He'll be out tomorrow." Honey jerked her head toward the bathroom floor. Sadie twisted to see a laptop lying on the tiles, open to Facebook Messenger. Eighteen new notifications.

Honey rubbed the flannel harder into Sadie's cheek, smearing black and red blood. "You didn't even *try* to make it nice for him, by the way."

"I still can't figure out how to do the venom, okay? I get too into it." Sadie took Honey's wrist, halting her harsh rubbing. She leaned in and sucked on the flannel, tasting soap and tap water and a few drops of lukewarm blood.

"Ew, Jesus, *stop*." Honey reached down and produced a bright pink thermos. She twisted the cap off, and Sadie's eagerness faded to resignation as the scent wafted out.

"Raccoon," Honey said. She tilted the thermos, letting Sadie see the warm blood slosh around the metal tube.

Sadie made a face.

Honey groaned. "Don't be a baby! God. I was *not* this bad in my first week."

"I had to stab you with a piece of mirror," Sadie reminded her weakly.

"Whatever. Can't *wait* until your restraint kicks in." Honey swabbed Sadie's neck, surprisingly gentle along her stark collarbones.

Sadie drank from the thermos, trying not to focus on the numb spot at the back of her head. She hoped her skull wasn't open. She *really* hoped Honey didn't take close-up pictures. She used to do that sometimes when they got injured, then excitedly show Sadie while she dry-heaved.

Sadie finished the thermos with a grimace. "How bad is it?"

Honey hummed so high the next words were guaranteed to be a lie. "Not that bad."

"Great," Sadie said flatly.

They froze. Footsteps echoed down the hall.

"Crap," Honey said. She grabbed a towel and tossed it over Sadie's sticky hair. Her laptop dinged in the background with yet another Facebook notification.

Sadie sat on the thermos. "What do we say?"

"Just..." Honey trailed off into a wince as the door-knob jiggled, the lock holding steady.

"Honey," called Bree Williams wearily. "That'd better be you, otherwise we have some very incompetent burglars."

"Better than competent ones," Honey called.

"You didn't drop by when you came in. I told you to say hi when you got home, even if I was asleep."

Honey rolled her eyes hard. "*Hiiiii* mom!"

Sadie picked at her towel. There was something wet and sticky at the back of her neck. She reached to wipe it off, only realizing that might be a bad idea when she pulled her hand back and found a lump of flesh with hair on it, like she'd just picked up a piece of her own scalp.

"EW NO OH MY GOD!" Sadie flung the disgusting handful to the other end of the bathtub, where it landed with a *splat.*

Honey froze. Sadie didn't freeze with her, too busy wiping her hand on the towel.

"Is someone in there with you?" The doorknob rattled again. "Wait a second, I know that shriek. Honey! Open this door and let me say hi to Sadie!"

Honey glared. Sadie glared back, still wiping the black chunks off her hand.

"Sorry I freaked out about touching my own detached *scalp,*" she hissed.

"Get over it, I barely nicked you!" Honey jerked the towel so it covered Sadie's eyes and got up reluctantly to let her mom in.

Bree shuffled in with a tired grin. Her teeth were oddly white thanks to a mishap with teeth whitening strips, but otherwise it was the same smile Sadie had been on the receiving end of for so many years: wide and warm with too much gum. A white negligee hung loose at Bree's hips, strawberry blonde curls bouncing against her freckled shoulders. She waved, and Sadie was struck by the mortifying realization that yes, she definitely had a crush on Honey's mom while they were growing up.

"Mom, Sadie, Sadie, Mom," Honey said, rushed. "There, you've seen her. Can we get back to it now?"

Bree ignored her, coming to sit on the lip of the bathtub and picking at Sadie's dirt-streaked shirt. "You look awful. What the hell did you two get up to on that road trip?"

Sadie laughed awkwardly, averting her eyes like Bree might see all the bloody motel bathrooms and underage clubbing and murder if she looked close enough. Not to mention the open head wound under the towel.

Bree frowned, coaxing Honey closer so she could tweak her dirty hair. "Honey! It's the day before school, we don't have time to fix this!"

"It just needs a few washes, Mom. Quit freaking out." Honey gave Sadie an exasperated look that catapulted her right back to childhood: they'd been in this scenario before, Honey giving them both a bad dye job the day before they went back from Christmas break in fourth grade. Honey had arrived halfway through the school day with her hair back to normal, and she'd dragged Sadie over to her house to dye it again before the week was out.

Bree dabbed at the black goo staining Sadie's sleeve. "What even *is* this? Did you go roll in some...alien goo?"

"Wrong genre, mom. We're in a really fucked-up romcom." Honey rested her head on Bree's shoulder, digging her chin in. "Get out please!"

"I'm getting, I'm getting. *Excuse* me for trying to catch up with Sadie after all these years." Bree huffed and stood, hand hovering over Sadie's shoulder like she wanted to squeeze it but didn't want to risk the muck. Her smile was still warm, and Sadie shrank underneath it. Nobody had looked at her like that since she started failing tests and wearing baggy clothes. It filled her with a strange sense of dread. Like it was only a matter of time before she let Bree down.

"It's so nice seeing you two having sleepovers again," Bree said. "I can't wait to tell the girls at work—"

Honey cut her off. "Don't."

Bree blinked, confused at the panic in Honey's voice. Honey looked over at Sadie with a pointed stare as she wiped her cheek where the blood used to be. The blood Sadie had tried to lick off a few minutes ago.

Sadie's cold heart sank. The man she'd attacked was alive. It was dark, but he had to have seen *something*. If she and Honey started spending time together, people might put those pieces together. People would already gossip like crazy *without* anybody getting attacked. Honey and Sadie had been laughing about it on the ride back into town.

*Best gal pals back together*, Honey had said, grazing a finger over Sadie's mouth while she drove, pulling away when Sadie tried to bite it. *I'm gonna make you cool, just you wait. You'll be dating this year's prom queen.*

Sadie waited until Bree was gone. Honey knelt beside the bathtub again.

"Did he see us?"

Honey sighed, wiping grit from Sadie's arms. "He didn't have his night vision goggles when you ran at him, so...kinda. So far he's saying it was two girls. I don't know how much description he's giving the cops, but I'm gonna bet he'll shut up pretty fast. Cops will think he's crazy, saying all this crap."

Sadie laughed shakily. *"It was two teenage girls from hell, officer!"*

*"One of them bit me and the other one tackled her and smacked her with a rock until she stopped moving,"* Honey said in a nasally voice that made Sadie remember she had actually met Summer and Ken Lu's dad, while she was waiting to get picked up after school on the rainiest day in freshman year. He'd asked Summer what she'd done that day, his nasally voice attentive and kind. He'd brought her an umbrella so she didn't get wet running to the parking lot. Sadie's fifteen-year-old self had ached for her mom. She'd sat there for another two hours before her dad finally pulled up, apologizing about missing her texts and not saying another word for the rest of the ride home.

Honey pulled Sadie's face closer. Sadie moved obediently, and Honey rubbed the washcloth around her ears.

Sadie squirmed. "Oh my god, I can *shower.*"

"I'm just being attentive," Honey complained, pinching her cheek. "Don't you want an attentive girl-friend? Do you want me to leave you to clean your own weird vampire blood off of you when half your skull is showing?"

"'S not *half*," Sadie protested.

Honey kept rubbing her ears. She looked oddly flustered.

"What?"

Honey shook her head. "We're, like...we're *girl-friends*, right? I mean, obviously we can't be *open* now. I know we were gonna, but if we can't even tell people we're *friends*..."

Sadie grinned. Honey looked so *sweet*, all bumbling and nervous. She only got like this around something she really, really wanted.

Honey *wanted* Sadie. Years without talking and she'd broken into Sadie's house to invite her on a murderous road trip. She'd kissed her blood into Sadie's mouth, turning it into a lifeblood that brought Sadie back to her.

Sadie leaned in. Honey made a noise, soft and pleased, against her mouth. She tasted like iron and earth and the faintest trace of lip gloss. Her eyelashes fluttered as Sadie drew back, still self-conscious in a way Sadie rarely saw. The washcloth was draped around her wrist, forgotten.

Sadie tapped the freckles dotting Honey's nose. "You're so cute when you're nervous!"

"Shut up." Honey batted her hand away, then mimed biting it.

A scary thought made Sadie pull back. "The cops won't come looking for us, right?"

"I told you, Mr. Lu didn't—"

"No, like...back..." Sadie stared at her until it clicked.

"No," Honey said. "Reddit says—"

"Oh, if *Reddit* says—"

"Shut up. Reddit says the cops are looking for the bassist." Honey leaned over, closing her laptop. "There still aren't a lot of articles out. Everyone's being really quiet. There are already conspiracies."

"Unless they try to drag us into it, I don't care." Sadie sighed, sagging against Honey's shoulder. Honey remained strangely quiet for so long Sadie looked up. "Wait, *are* they dragging us into it? I know we ran off stage, but none of the articles mentioned us, so—"

"What?" Honey blinked, distracted. "No, nobody's said shit about us. I just..."

She trailed off. Two vulnerable silences in one conversation. It was a night for miracles.

Sadie dug her chin into Honey's shoulder. Honey groaned reflexively, as if that could hurt her anymore.

"It's nothing," Honey said in response to Sadie's silent question. She let out a small, nervous laugh. "I kinda feel like I ruined your life a little bit."

Sadie thought back to her life one month ago. In the guts of summer vacation, slowly becoming one with the couch, on another endless cycle of reruns and shoplifted vodka. Not talking to anyone for days at a time. The world narrowing into that shitty little living room, population: Sadie Greer.

The world was bigger now. Scarier and infinitely

more uncertain—but *bigger*. She had her favorite person back, even if they were bound by a ravenous secret they couldn't tell anyone about. Sure, Sadie had gone feral and ruined their chances of hanging out together. Sure, Sadie's hunger still wasn't calming down like Honey's did. Sure, the future was uncertain and filled with terrors.

But she wasn't alone anymore. She had Honey. *That's* what mattered.

Sadie ignored the howling in her stomach and smiled.

"You didn't ruin anything," she said. She took Honey's hand, their joined skin as cool as the bathtub porcelain. "I'm so happy to be here. Even with all the..."

She gestured down at herself, all the viscera left to clean up. "I'd still take my life now over the boring shit-show of three weeks ago."

Honey snorted. She still looked uncertain, but it was hard to notice when she was smiling so prettily.

"Of course you'd take this life," she said, affection softening her proud tone. "It's got *me*."

chapter
**two**

SCHOOL WAS *LOUD*. Lockers slamming, bored pencils tapping, paper being folded into notes to pass across the classroom. Constant chatter, enough to make Honey's head ache.

The whispers were loudest in the cafeteria. Among all the forks scraping and chairs dragging in and out, and Summer and Britney on either side of Honey whining about their biology homework, people whispered:

*"Can't imagine Mr. Lu on drugs."*

*"I heard it was homeless people."*

*"No way a person could make those bites, he was all ripped up!"*

Honey toyed with her juice box straw, making eye contact with Sadie from across the cafeteria. So fast and fleeting it would've looked like an accident to anybody watching.

Sadie sat at her usual empty table tucked in the corner of the cafeteria. Her shoulders were tight under her hoodie, hair messy underneath her cap. Her skin was paler than yesterday. Apart from one single red apple, her cafeteria tray was empty.

"Mom's already making me narrow down my top three colleges," Summer said, loud enough to jerk Honey's attention back to the table. "Like, calm down, right? I'll be happy if I get into my safety schools, I don't *have* a top three."

She twisted one of her pigtails around her hand, a bored habit that boys liked to mistake as a come-on. She'd blown up Honey's Facebook messenger with texts last night, but this morning she'd been over it. Once it sunk in that her dad really was going to be fine, she was just annoyed that he couldn't drive her to the next town for a shopping trip this weekend.

Next to her, Britney scoffed. "I can't believe your mom let you wait until senior year. *My* parents made me start picking colleges when I was a freshman." She snapped her cherry-flavored gum. Yet another method of controlling her perfectly reasonable appetite. Britney had been copying Honey for years—adopting her fashion sense, her giggle, even her posture. She would do anything to make herself look like Honey except gain weight. Britney was convinced she could be a better version of her: Honey, but *thin*. She was the kind of person who thought thinness automatically made you better.

Britney turned to Honey, jaw working around her

cherry gum. "Where are you applying, Honey? Community college?"

It was the first thing she'd said to Honey since she sat down. She'd been weirdly distant today in a way that made Honey think she was hiding something. The last time Britney had been this evasive, she'd stolen Honey's favorite shoes and tried to convince her that they were a brand new but eerily similar pair.

Honey twisted her straw hard. She thought about telling Britney about her newfound bloodlust. Would that be the line that Britney wouldn't cross in her imitation of Honey, or would she buy a set of Halloween fangs?

"I have a 4.0 GPA, Brit. I'm in AP classes, Brit. I'm a *very* pretty face, but you do know I'm smart, right?"

"Well, you just...you never..." Britney looked beseechingly at Summer, who instantly took up the opportunity to smooth things over.

"What do you want to major in?"

Honey thought about it.

"Fashion," she lied.

Summer and Britney nodded sagely. Behind them, more whispers trickled into Honey's ears.

*"Nobody could get in touch with Honey for literal weeks. Who knows what she was doing?"*

*"Just don't believe she'd ever be friends with—"*

"Um," said a voice directly in front of her. "Honey?"

Honey's gaze snapped up. She looked into the annoyed face of Ken Lu, who had technically started this whole mess. If he hadn't been so annoying at that party, she never would have annoyed him back by getting into The Bleeding Bastards' van.

"What the hell, babe? You never texted me back. What gives?"

Behind him, crammed in that tiny table in the corner, Sadie snorted. Honey made a mental note to rib her later for eavesdropping.

"Honestly I kind of forgot you existed," Honey replied, as Summer and Britney watched shamelessly. "Didn't you go home with that cheerleader from East High?"

"What? No. Jesus." Ken shifted uncomfortably. "Wouldn't actually do that to you, babe. I just, y'know. Made it look like that. Like you made it look like you got with that band. I know you didn't."

"I didn't," Honey confirmed. "But don't call me *babe*. We're not together."

Ken scoffed. He scratched his head with his whole arm behind his back, which he only did to show off his arm muscles.

"Come on. Don't be like that."

"Seriously? I didn't text you back for two weeks! Get a clue!" Honey tinkled her fingers at him. "Bye, Ken. Good luck finding someone else to sing at your birthday party this weekend."

The last part was a lie. She would show up no matter what. But she still wanted to mess with him a little. Maybe make him beg.

Ken tugged anxiously at his puka shell necklace. He'd started off wearing it ironically, then it became a thing people knew him by—*that guy with the big hair and the puka shell necklace*—and it was too late to stop.

Honey kept waving. Summer and Britney turned to join in, Summer with that perfect lazy flap, Britney too excited as always.

"Bye, bro," Summer crooned.

Ken scowled.

"Whatever," he told Honey. "Hope you had a good time killing that boy band with your burnout bestie."

Honey froze. Over Ken's shoulder, so did Sadie.

Ken stormed off, muttering things Honey would've preferred not to overhear. She fixed her smile back into place and turned to her friends, letting out a bewildered laugh.

"What? Did he have a *stroke*? Killing a boy band with my burnout bestie, what does *that* mean?"

Summer and Britney suddenly developed a keen interest in their own fingernails.

Honey pinched Summer's wrist. "Hey! What the hell was your shithead brother talking about?"

Summer and Britney traded looks, rubbing their sore wrists. Honey had perhaps pinched them harder than she should have.

"There's this video," Summer started. "By this true crime YouTuber."

"Everyone's been sending it around," Britney added, speaking way too fast. "There's, like, a photo. It *does* look a lot like you and Sadie. You two used to hang out, right?"

Honey's eyes itched with how much she wanted to look at Sadie, drink in the sight of that pale face and tired eyes, dark hair shoved into that cap to hide the gory hole in her head. To look over and know they were both thinking of that dirty bathroom, Honey kissing her own blood into Sadie's mouth. *Don't make me lose you. We just got each other back.*

"Like a million years ago," Honey said.

They had five minutes until the bell rang.

Honey sat on the closed toilet lid, Sadie leaning over her shoulder with her arm resting awkwardly on the toilet paper dispenser.

"You *need* to buy a new phone," Sadie told her as Honey typed into the search bar.

Honey shushed her and clicked on the video: ***YOU WON'T BELIEVE THIS UPDATE ON THE BLEEDING BASTARDS SLAUGHTER!!!!*** by spookytimegirlies04.

A young Korean American woman appeared onscreen, smiling wide. She had a butterfly clip in her smooth, shiny hair and a drawn-on heart decorating her chubby cheeks. The video quality was good, but the lighting was shoddy. Too bright on her face and too dark everywhere else, washing her out while leaving the room in shadow.

"What's *up*, my spooky time girlies," the woman said. "If you're new here, my name is Clarissa and I have an exciting update on our new case!"

"Case," Honey repeated. "What is she, a detective? You're like nineteen years old and clearly live in your childhood bedroom, go get a job."

Clarissa continued, "One of my beautiful little commenters got in touch saying they were actually at that show and they have a photo of the opening band that ran off stage and *vanished* right before The Bleeding Bastards got locked in the bathroom and murdered. Super sus, right?"

She snapped her fingers. A photo appeared onscreen, blurred and grainy: two girls on a stage. A thin dark smudge of a girl holding a guitar and a big girl with a shiny ponytail grinning against a microphone.

Their faces were partially obscured—Sadie's by her hair, Honey's by the stage lights. The only thing visible was their smiles, bright and blazing. They looked like they were having the time of their lives.

Honey's cold heart squeezed. That snapshot was everything she dreamed of as a kid. Her and Sadie on the stage, taking on the world.

She forced her face into a bored expression and leaned back. "At least it's a hot photo."

Sadie groaned. "It's *us*."

"It's not obviously us—"

"*Everybody's* seen me wear that shirt, Hon!"

"There are a lot of shitty flannels in the world," Honey mumbled.

Clarissa was still talking. "Journalists had to STRUGGLE to get any information out of the cops, NOBODY is talking about this! To anybody who needed a recap, The Bleeding Bastards were supposed to play a set last week in—"

"We *know*," Sadie said. She leaned over Honey to steal her phone back.

Honey yanked it out of her reach. "Wait! She posted a new video ten minutes ago!"

"Okay, so—" Sadie fell silent as Honey shoved the phone in her face. The thumbnail proclaimed: ***BLEEDING BASTARDS MURDERERS FOUND IN TENNESSEE???*** with Clarissa open-mouthed next to two blacked-out photos.

Honey swallowed. "Maybe there are two other suspects in Tennessee?"

Sadie glared at her and clicked play, fast-forwarding past the introductions.

"A lovely commenter got in touch saying they know those girls," Clarissa said excitedly.

A comment appeared onscreen, timestamped from last night.


***itsbritneybitch006:***

*you will not BELIEVE what i'm about to say. first off:*

*those girls went to my middle school!! they were in a band when they were younger, my school website has pics*

A photograph appeared: Honey and Sadie in all their twelve-year-old glory, Honey on a microphone, Sadie on a guitar, looking eerily similar to that blurry photo in the previous video.

"Britney you BITCH," Honey shrieked.

Sadie shushed her. Britney's comment continued:

*second: my friend's dad JUST got attacked in the woods LEGIT TWENTY MINUTES AGO. guess what he's saying?? he said TWO GIRLS BIT HIM??? WITH THEIR TEETH?? cops are saying he's on drugs bc it looks like an ANIMAL BITE!!!! idk about guitarist but the singer hasn't replied to anyone's texts in weeks wtf is happeninggggg do we have some CREATURES in my stupid little hometown??? everybody get ur pitchforks lmaooo*

"This is *wild*," Clarissa continued. "Do these two girls have something to do with the murders? Are we looking at some cryptid shit? God, I hope so. Anyway, here are some photos of the girls she's talking about."

Two more photos appeared onscreen. Honey and

Sadie watched in appalled silence as Clarissa continued reading out comments.

It was their yearbook photos from last year. Sadie in that same flannel shirt she was wearing in the Honeybloods photo, scowling hard. And Honey in a pink hoodie decorated with hearts, dimples showing, shooting the camera a flirty wink.

Honey sighed. "Shit."

chapter<br>three

SADIE WASN'T USED to being stared at.

She wasn't a troublemaker. She wasn't a rebel, flipping off teachers and getting into fights. She was a *burnout,* skipping class and staying quiet and blending into the background. She was a hazy blip on the edges of her classmates' radar. Nobody remembered her long enough to make fun of her.

Until today. Sadie pulled her baseball cap down and hunched over her quiz paper, concentrating on her pencil scratching. If she focused hard enough, she couldn't hear all the whispers, the near-silent tap of fingers on phone screens. Her neck prickled with the weight of everyone glancing at her. Her stomach twisted with hunger despite all those thermoses of animal blood Honey had brought her last night, feeding Sadie in the bathtub until she could walk around without falling over.

The bell rang. Sadie flinched, scrabbling for her backpack.

Mr. Halbert clapped his hands. "Hey! Everybody going for your bags: who dismisses you, me or the bell?"

"You do," the class droned, automatic.

"That's right. You can go once you've finished your quiz."

Sadie slumped back into her seat. She was one of a small number of students staying in their seats. Officially, the quiz would let Mr. Halbert know what he needed to teach this year. Unofficially, it would tell him who he needed to give up on.

Ken Lu bumped into Sadie's desk as he crossed the classroom, coming to a stop in front of Honey. Sadie watched them out of the corner of her eye, saying nothing. *Please have him be butthurt about the breakup, please don't let him bring up that stupid YouTube video.*

"So," Ken started, smug and delighted. "Did you bite my dad?"

"Oh yeah." Honey licked her lips. "Yum."

Summer groaned from the classroom doorway. Beside her, Britney stopped with a nervous grin. She'd been eyeing Honey all through class, once Honey found out it was her comments that led to the YouTube accusations.

"Jesus, Ken," Summer snapped, ignoring all the students lining up behind her to get out. "He took it all back!"

"Sure," Ken said, not taking his eyes off Honey.

"He was in *shock*," Summer protested. "It was dark! People see all sorts of things in the dark. Leave Honey alone, you little freak."

"Yeah, Ken. Leave her alone." Britney's lips pursed in a smug smile.

It faded fast as Honey cleared her throat.

"Surprised you'd say that, Brit. Since it was you who pointed that YouTube weirdo toward me."

"Um," Britney said, so high-pitched that Sadie winced. "I don't...that wasn't..."

She sped toward the exit. Summer followed, sending Honey a wide-eyed look that promised they were going to talk about this at *length* later. Other classmates milled into the hallway after them, looking reluctant to leave what was sure to be great gossip fodder.

"I texted my mom," Ken told Honey, toying with his puka shell necklace in a way that made Sadie want to strangle him with it. "You're still singing at my party on Friday."

Honey stopped packing her books into her bag. Sadie knew how Honey's face would look: that fake incredulity hiding the deep eagerness at the prospect of tearing someone down.

"Does your mom know I *dumped* you?"

"She still paid you the deposit."

"I can give it back," Honey said, sweet and mocking. "I'm not a *business*. I'm a hot girl who stayed in choir too long and did *one* jingle for a local radio station."

Sadie kept her eyes on her quiz, which she'd wholeheartedly given up on. Let Mr. Halbert fail her. She wasn't the only one killing time to listen in on this conversation—some of her classmates were tying already-tied shoes or pretending to be engrossed in their phones.

Ken sighed. "Look, you know how my mom is. If you don't sing, then that means you're not cool with me in some way. I've lied to her for years about being friends with all my exes, and I'm not losing that streak because of one crazy bitch."

Sadie bit her cheek to stop a laugh. Someone on the other side of the room wasn't so lucky, letting out a snort. It sounded like Mr. Halbert, who was pretending to ignore them as he played Tetris on his phone.

"I'll sing," Honey said. "If you beg."

Ken ran his tongue over his teeth.

Honey cocked her head. "Come on, Ken. Kenny-benny. Baby boy. I want to hear you beg."

Sadie had to force her gaze to stay on her paper. She couldn't look up, no matter how badly she wanted to see Honey take this guy down a peg.

"Please," Ken said with a strained smile. "Get my mom off my ass."

"I'd love to," Honey said, half-sunny, half-sneer. "Tell your mom I need a fog machine."

Ken sniggered. "Wow. Perform before *one* real band and you get *really* up yourself."

People were stopping in the hall. Sadie could hear them lingering near the classroom door, whispering, texting, eager to get the latest and weirdest gossip.

Honey twisted toward the door. "I know there's not a lot to do in this town," she called. "But I didn't know we were bored enough to jump onto murder conspiracy theories about shitty emo bands!"

"You didn't think they were so shitty when you got in their van." Ken flashed his stupid blunt teeth. "What'd you do, follow them to New Orleans?"

"Sure, Ken. Then I *cut their heads off with an ax.*" Honey held up her hands, nails freshly cleaned and polished after she'd finished wiping blood from Sadie's hair. "Do these look like ax-chopping hands? I was at my aunt's place in Memphis, dumbass. You can ask my mom. Anyway, *everyone* knows it was the bassist. Why else would he run off and go into hiding?"

Ken grunted. Sadie listened to his gleaming white Nikes cross the classroom and hoped he was heading for the door, tail between his legs. It would be the fastest he ever gave in to Honey, but maybe they were just lucky today. Maybe—

"Sadie," Ken said, leaning against her desk. "Where were *you* for the past two weeks? Cashier at Cooper's Corner says he didn't see you skulking around the liquor section. Suspicious."

He gave the rest of the classroom a grin, waggling his eyebrows at the people lingering out in the hall. The crowd was growing, everyone wanting to hear about the strange internet rumor.

"You guys were in that talent show in middle school, right? You played guitar. She sang. Called yourselves..."

Ken pressed his hands over her quiz paper. "What was it? *Honeybabes*. Just like those girls."

"That wasn't our name," Sadie said stiffly.

There were already arguments in the comments section about what the mysterious band had been called versus what the two suspects had named their band in middle school. Like a game of telephone between a guy watching an opening band in a bar last week and a bunch of teenagers who sat through a talent show four years ago.

Sadie eyed Ken's hands pressed flat against her quiz paper. A vein twisted up around his palm, curving around the meat of his thumb. She was so *hungry*, even with all that raccoon blood she'd choked down in Honey's bathtub.

Sadie pushed her cap back to fix him with a withering stare. "You really think it's a smart idea to piss off a girl if you think she chopped up three grown men in a bathroom?"

Silence fell. Even Mr. Halbert paused behind his desk where he'd been fiddling with his briefcase clip for the last thirty seconds. Sadie's classmates hadn't heard her speak in a long time.

Honey sniggered. "Oooo-*kay*, freak."

Everyone laughed. Sadie imagined ripping their necks open. Pinning Ken down, taking one side of his neck while Honey took the other. Biting harder when he shrieked.

Honey stood with a flourish. "I don't know what this

flannel-wearing freak was doing on summer break, but *I* was getting mani pedis and drinking champagne with my coolest, richest aunt. And if any delusional true crime losers come looking for me because of my asshole friend's YouTube comments, I will sneak into the house of every single person who liked her comment and put lye in your shampoo. Toodles, bitches!"

More laughter. More whispers. Old betrayal raged through Sadie's stomach even though she knew it was fake, even though Honey had wiped raccoon blood so tenderly from her mouth last night.

Sadie reminded herself of Honey's flustered expression when she asked Sadie if they were girlfriends. It didn't make it hurt any less when Honey ignored her as she strode out.


The fake betrayal was still simmering in her empty stomach as she waited, motionless, on her own bed. She did this a lot: lying here, staring at nothing. It always ended the same way.

Her hand snaked under her mattress. She pulled out the bottle of vodka she'd stashed several weeks ago while Honey was yelling for her to hurry up and come help her bury a body. She held it up to the light, watching the sun filter through the plastic. The last time she held this bottle, she had no friends. No future. No howling hunger in her gut. Not for blood, anyway.

She uncapped the bottle and took a swig. Relief

washed over her in a wave, even as she fought the urge to gag. It was so *cold*, and it tasted different than usual. Less like chemicals and more like sludge. She tipped the bottle back and drank until it was empty, no breath to hold her back. She could apocalyptically wasted or she'd puke a fountain of vodka. Either way, she wanted to go all in.

The relief faded. Sadie sat back, waiting for the head rush. That first-drink feeling that everything would be okay.

It didn't come.

What did come was vomit. A *lot* of vomit. Sadie was bent over the toilet heaving another string of black bile into the bowl when she heard a car pull up outside.

The front door slammed. Honey's voice echoed through the house: "She's gonna drop me off a block away next time! I got her on board with the cover story, you're welcooooome. And I got a phone! Everything's coming up Milhouse!"

Sadie groaned into the toilet bowl.

Honey stopped yelling. The sound of platform boots thudded down the hallway, because Sadie's house didn't have a Shoes Off At The Door policy, unlike her own.

Honey appeared in the doorway, new phone dangling from her hand. "What, did you see a burger and just had to—oh, wow, this room *reeks* of booze."

Sadie flipped her off. Honey darted forward to twist her finger, then patted the back of Sadie's head. "Looks like most of your scalp is back. Now you just gotta regrow the hair."

With that, she sat down next to her on the bathroom floor.

"We spend too much time hanging out in bathrooms," Sadie croaked. She lifted her head off the toilet lid. "Your mom's on board? Did she see—"

"Oh, yeah." Honey tweaked Sadie's bangs, lifting them out of her eyes. "I told her we snuck into a bar and lied our way into playing a set. Ran off stage because we saw security coming."

"And she didn't *ground* you?"

"No, she did." Honey beamed, and the sight was so stupidly beautiful that for one moment, Sadie forgot she was hungry. "No leaving the house except for Ken's birthday party, since I'm getting paid. And seeing *you*. She's so happy we're friends again that she drove me over. She does *not* like my other friends."

"They *are* pretty awful," Sadie agreed.

Honey's jaw worked. She wanted to apologize for the classroom, Sadie could tell. But she hated apologizing, so she'd just say something sweet until Sadie forgave her.

"That used to be the big guns," Honey said, sitting there on Sadie's bathroom floor while her skirt collected the dust. Sadie and her dad hadn't vacuumed in here since her mom left.

"*No more Sadie*," Honey continued. "She only pulled that out when I did something really, really naughty."

"You stole her credit card," Sadie mumbled. "She didn't let us see each other for two weeks."

Sadie waited for the forgiveness to arrive, but the sting of betrayal from the classroom stuck in her like a shard of glass. She convulsed. Nothing came up.

Honey wrinkled her nose. "Gross, babe."

"Don't *babe*. We're not a *babe* couple."

"Excuse you. *You* don't get to choose what pet names I give you." Honey rested her chin on Sadie's shoulder, keeping it there when Sadie tried to shrug her off. "What'd you think, food's a bust but liquids are a pass? Rookie mistake, *babe*."

Sadie stared into the toilet bowl, all that thick black goo. "I just...I wanted..."

She squeezed her eyes shut. She didn't want to tell Honey about the huge, irrational need she had for liquor sometimes, desperate and numb. She used to think she liked being drunk, but over the years she realized she liked the actual act of drinking. The relief of that first sip, before any physical change even took place—it felt like coming up for air. Like a starving man eating a feast. Even now, with no chemical effect whatsoever, that relief had still come. She could rely on that, at least.

"I need to go hunting again," she rasped.

Honey made a dubious noise, going through her phone. "I can do it. I'll bring a sack of thermoses. All the thermoses we got."

Sadie lifted her head. Honey kept scrolling through her phone.

"You think I'm gonna eat somebody again?"

"Ummm," Honey said. "*Yes*? You're still new."

"You have *one* week on me." Sadie chewed her cheek, tasting vodka and vomit. "Maybe this is just—"

Honey gasped, shoving her phone in Sadie's face. *New video from spookytimegirlies04,* proclaimed her YouTube notifications. ***MORE INFO ON THE TENNESSEE HONEYBABES!! DON'T MISS THIS ONE >>>>>***

Sadie pushed herself up. "Oh, great. At least she got the name wrong again."

Honey didn't answer. Her head was cocked, eyes tracking. Listening.

Sadie scrolled through the video comments, scowling. "Next she's gonna show up at our houses."

Honey hummed. It was a very pointed hum, her eyes still tracking nothing as she listened. "Somebody's at the door."

"Huh?"

Three light knocks echoed through the house.

Sadie looked at Honey, who was twirling her hair pointedly.

"If it's spookytimegirlies04," Sadie announced, "I *will* bite her."

"Dibs," Honey said, and stood.

chapter
**four**

SADIE WATCHED Clarissa through the peephole.

Gone were the butterfly clips. Gone, too, were the tiny hearts studded on her plump cheeks. Her shiny black hair was pulled back in a sensible ponytail, a smart white blouse buttoned up to her neck. She was wearing a blazer it was too hot for, and glasses that looked like they'd been picked up at a drugstore on the way here. She was wearing *suspenders*.

Honey whispered, "Do you think she typed *detective chic* into Google Images and just went with the first hit?"

Sadie shushed her. On the front porch, Clarissa perked up.

"Um, hello," she called. "I'd like to talk to Sadie Greer? I'm not a telemarketer, I promise!"

"I say you let her in," Honey whispered.

Sadie gaped at her.

Honey shrugged. "Set the story straight or whatever. *No, officer, I was nowhere near that bar. I was sitting at home watching* Gilmore Girls *and getting party girl wasted.*"

"I can hear somebody," Clarissa called. She fidgeted with her suspenders, wincing when the band snapped back into her chest. "Ow."

"I'll hide in your room," Honey hissed. "You haven't talked to me in years, you were here the whole summer. Go go go!"

Sadie swatted at her. Honey ducked it, blurring down the hall and vanishing into Sadie's bedroom. Sadie spared a moment to be embarrassed about the state of it —clothes strewn over the floor, trashcan overflowing, a hundred forgotten notes and abandoned assignments crammed into drawers—before she opened the door.

Clarissa blinked. "Hi guys," she said, breaking into that giant smile Sadie recognized from the YouTue videos. It wobbled, like she wasn't used to doing it away from the camera. She peered behind Sadie at the empty living room. "I mean, guy. Sorry, I thought there was somebody else here."

"I was talking to myself," Sadie lied. "I was giving myself a pep talk before opening the door."

Clarissa laughed, high and nervous. "I get that! Before I hand my resume in anyplace, I stand in front of my mirror and tell myself I'm amazing and hot and funny, you know? Then usually they tell me to apply online! Not that I've been applying for a lot of jobs lately."

She trailed off. Then she curtsied, a movement that

started out ironic then turned serious halfway through. "I'm, um, Clarissa? This might sound super weird, but I'm—"

"Spookytimegirlies04. I know."

Clarissa's light brown eyes lit up. "Yes, oh my god! And you're Sadie Greer! This is honestly so flattering, I've never been *recognized* before."

She looked so genuinely pleased, it was difficult to hate her. Sadie tried anyway.

"How'd you get my address?"

"Oh, someone in your school DM'd me."

"Who?"

"Um, Britney...somebody. I don't know her last name." Clarissa scratched her thin wrists, the veins pulsing hard underneath. "Can I come in?"

Sadie thought very hard about slamming the door in her face. Then she remembered Honey hiding in her room listening to every word.

"Sure," she said icily, and headed toward the living room couch.

Clarissa stepped in daintily. At first she left the door open, then she whirled to close it like an afterthought. She moved like a ballerina who had quit a few years ago due to a growth spurt, both graceful and gangly.

She held out her phone hopefully. "Do you mind if I record this conversation?"

"Yes." Sadie sat on the couch and stared until Clarissa slid the phone back into her blazer.

"Do you have any other recording devices?"

Clarissa shook her head and perched at the other end of the couch. "I thought about wearing a wire. But who am I, CSI Miami? Right? Anyway, don't worry, I know how weird this is. I just—I live three hours away and when Britney gave me your address I just thought, what the hell! Hopped in my trusty Honda Civic and drove right over."

She laughed again. She'd smeared cinnamon deodorant on her pits and wrists. Sadie could smell it from here. The nervous sweat bled through anyway, dampening the blazer it was too hot for.

"Weird thing to do if you think I killed someone," Sadie told her.

Clarissa gasped, hand flying to her face and smacking herself right in the glasses she obviously wasn't used to wearing. "Oh, I don't actually think you did it! This isn't about, like, *solving* the case, I'm not smart enough for that. And it sounds like a weird case, the cops aren't releasing much information so there's not much to go on. This is just a story for my channel. If I get a couple hundred more subscribers and some more watch hours, they start paying me and I can stop relying on my Patreon to pay my parents rent!"

Sadie couldn't think of anything to say to that except, "Your parents make you pay rent?"

Clarissa shrugged. Her blazer had shoulder pads. She took out her phone again, flipping through her photos. "Can you take a look at this for me?"

She held her phone out. Sadie stared at the grainy

photo of Honeybloods' first and likely only real performance, their joy so bright it almost made Sadie lose her composure and smile back at them.

She sat back, shaking her head. "That's not me. I was here all summer."

"Great! Do you have anyone to confirm that?"

"Nope."

"You didn't see any friends...coworkers...parents?"

"I'm a bit of a loner," Sadie said, her voice monotone. "My dad was on a job for most of that time, but he can confirm I was here the day of that show."

A low whisper drifted out from the hallway, so quiet Sadie had to strain her new super hearing: "*Ooooh, you're so hot when you're lying.*"

"I can say I haven't talked to Honey Williams for years," Sadie said loudly. "Couldn't pay me to play a show with her. What a stuck-up bitch."

Honey snickered from behind Sadie's bedroom door. Sadie chewed her cheek to stop a smile.

"Okay," Clarissa chirped, going to push a stray hair behind her ears and getting tangled up in her new glasses again. "Oof. Um, can you give me her number?"

"I don't have it," Sadie lied. Her phone sat guiltily in her jeans pocket, Honey's number cocooned by wink emojis, courtesy of all the times Honey stole her phone on the road trip. "Like I said, we don't hang out."

"Alright," Clarissa said. Sadie couldn't tell if she believed her. "So, about this guy who got attacked by two girls—"

"I thought it was a bear," Sadie blurted.

"Oh! Well, Britney said the guy was claiming it was two girls. So did the cashier at a gas station a few blocks away. Sooo."

*"I hate small towns,"* Honey whispered from Sadie's room.

Sadie silently agreed. *"I* heard they almost ripped his throat out. So unless these *girls* grew fangs..." She smiled stiffly, showing off her useless human teeth. "I'm pretty sure it was a bear. Or a really, really pissed off raccoon."

"But—" Clarissa cut off as the front door opened. Sadie's dad came to a dead halt in the middle of the doorway when he noticed Sadie wasn't alone.

Sadie waved. "Dad. Hey."

Munson Greer nodded, toying anxiously with his mustache. He was twenty years older than all the other dads, he was the town's second-best handyman, and he hadn't had company over at the house in years. Until recently, neither had Sadie.

Clarissa bolted up. "Hello! So nice to meet you. I'm—"

"Spookytimegirlies04," Sadie said over her, ignoring Clarissa's cringe and Munson's confused frown. "Dad, I was here all summer, right?"

She stared at him pointedly.

Munson Greer was not a demonstrative man. But sometimes when Sadie was having an obviously bad time —listening to screaming music, not leaving her bed for days—he'd wait until she wasn't crying, then he'd knock on the door and call through it: *Need anything?* If she said no (she always said no) he'd say, *I'd do anything for you. You know that, right?*

It was finally time to deliver.

Munson blinked. "Uh, sure. Us Greers aren't the type to go out and do stuff. Doing stuff is a fool's game. Safer to stay at home."

"Hear, hear," Sadie said.

Munson scratched his shirt awkwardly. "So. I'm gonna get started on dinner. You should get home."

Clarissa wavered, looking hopefully at Sadie. Sadie stared back, incredulous.

*"Take the hint,"* Honey whispered. *"Jeeeesus."*

"It was nice to meet you," Clarissa said. She skittered past Munson to the door, looking relieved. Sadie wondered if she'd give herself a reassuring pep talk in her car.

The door slid closed.

Sadie got up. "Well, I'm beat. I should—"

"What was that about? You in trouble?"

"When am I ever in trouble?" Sadie's butter-wouldn't-melt grin slid right off as he gave her a flat look. *"Other* than not turning in assignments, Dad. Come on."

He reached up, toying with the coat rack that was home to more spiderwebs than coats. "If you *are* in trouble—"

"You didn't tell anybody I was out of town, right?"

He snorted. "Sure. Told all my friends."

"Ha ha. Seriously, though."

He squinted at her, worry seeping through his perma-blank expression. "It didn't come up. Sadie—"

"It's nothing," she assured him. "There's this YouTube video and kids are being stupid about it. The point is: I was here all summer. Okay?"

"Alright," he said slowly. He scratched his shirt again. He got itchy when he was nervous.

Honey whispered from the bedroom: *"Can I come out now?"*

"No," Sadie said.

Munson frowned. "Huh?"

*"I'm coming out,"* Honey whispered. The bedroom door clicked open. "Helloooo! Do I hear a weird old man who only likes movies about underdogs excelling in sports, unless it's golf?"

"Golf is for wimps who make other people pick up their trash," Munson said, once he recovered from the shock of yet another person being in his house. He gave Sadie a questioning look, which Sadie steadfastly ignored.

Honey burst into the living room, posing against the doorframe like a pinup model. "Munson! I missed you. You look stunning, as usual."

"Uh-huh." Munson scratched harder at his shirt. There was a tiny hole in the white fabric, guaranteed to crop up in the stomach of every shirt he wore. "Didn't think I'd see you in this house again. Staying for dinner?"

"We were just leaving," Sadie said quickly, stalking over to Honey and giving her a pointed look.

Honey gave her one right back. "I think you mean *I* was just leaving. *You're* staying here until I get back."

Munson grunted. "You two having a sleepover?"

Honey beamed at him, ignoring Sadie's cutting glare. "Doing each other's hair and watching *Gilmore Girls*! Just like old times."

She started for the kitchen.

"I hate you," Sadie whispered.

"Choke on it," Honey whispered back. She winked, then turned so fast her hair smacked Sadie in the face. "Mr. Greer! May I have a thermos?"

Sadie stood at her bedroom window, watching Honey cross the street outside her house, a grocery bag filled with three thermoses dangling at her hip.

"Dad," she called. "You didn't see Honey here, either. We don't hang out."

There was a long pause.

"Got it," Munson called gruffly from the kitchen.

Sadie watched the grocery bag jostle against Honey's wide hip. She was pretty sure her dad wouldn't press her. He hadn't asked about her drinking, even after he found the stash of empties under her bed last year while helping strip her sheets. He hadn't asked about her grades after she almost failed out of freshman year. He didn't ask how she was doing after her mom left. He left her to her own devices, and she did the same for him.

Honey nodded at a man parked in a truck across the

road. The man tipped his hat, and Sadie frowned. She'd never seen that truck before, old and red and muddy, the windows blacked out. She'd never seen the man before, either, chewing a toothpick and fiddling with his cowboy hat. He had his window rolled down, watching Honey walk toward the woods.

Footsteps down the hall. Sadie turned to watch Munson stand awkwardly at her door, spatula in one hand, scratching that hole in his shirt.

"I could watch some of that *Gilmore Girls*," he offered. "While you're waiting for Honey."

"Thanks," Sadie said. "But I think I'm just gonna..."

She gestured uselessly around her room.

Munson nodded. "Got it. Well, you two have fun."

"Always do," Sadie said. She glanced back at the road. The truck was gone. Honey vanished into the woods across from Sadie's house, thermoses clinking at her side.

chapter
# **five**

HONEY PAUSED on her way up the back porch to run her tongue up the full thermos. Blood. Metal. The slightest musk from the possum she'd held upside down until it was drained dry.

She dropped the thermos back into her bag. It clinked against the other two, blood sloshing inside the metal tubes.

It would be enough, Honey told herself. Sadie was only this hungry because she was new and she was healing. After a few more days that hole in her head would be gone and the hunger would dial down from ravenous to irritating. Honey's hunger was nothing compared to those first few days, but the way Sadie had described it on the drive back made her think that maybe they were experiencing this *vampire* deal differently. Sure, Honey had been blinded by bloodlust. But only when she had her fangs in someone, and she could pull herself out of it now. Sadie's hunger sounded different: that deep, constant urge Sadie explained in the driver's seat while Honey nodded and tried not to look nervous.

She had her hand around the doorknob when her phone vibrated in her bra. She sighed, digging it out.

*You have one notification: spookytimegirlies04 has posted 2 new videos.*

Honey groaned.

The back door flew open, Sadie's cap almost whipping off with her speed. "Get in."

Honey pushed inside, pulling the door closed behind her.

Sadie asked, "Did you—"

"Yeah."

"I watched the first one while you were out."

"Bad?"

Sadie pinched her lips. She looked distracted.

Honey asked, "What?"

Sadie shook her head. Behind her, Munson clattered around in the kitchen, muttering. "Sonofabitch boys... nothing to do in this town, let's go yell at the Greer girl..."

"It's nothing," Sadie said, too fast. She twisted her septum piercing. "Some guys just egged the house."

A venomous, protective rage surged in Honey in ways it hadn't since middle school. Watching Sadie get stabbed in that dingy bathroom had been all horror and desperation. This was fury, hot and preemptively satisfying. Whenever Honey got this kind of mad, it would inevitably lead to a victory over whoever had screwed with Sadie.

"Who?" Honey snapped, stomping toward the front door. "If it's Ken, I am going to spread eight hundred rumors about how weird he is in bed—"

Sadie caught her arm before she could even get to the end of the hall. "What happened to not letting anyone see us together?"

"Your dad said they yelled. What'd they yell?"

"It doesn't matter," Sadie snapped. Her gaze flickered down to the bag clinking against Honey's hip.

"Shit, right." Honey dragged Sadie into her bedroom. *Bless Munson for listening to me and Sadie's bullshit excuses about privacy in grade school,* she thought as she locked the door behind them. They'd had him install the locks so they could play knifey fingers without fear of being walked in on.

Honey emptied the bag on Sadie's bed. "So I got a mix. Only tiny critters this time, no handy deer hanging around to..."

She trailed off as Sadie lunged for the nearest thermos—a small, battered black one Honey'd had to rinse dust out of before adding it to the collection—and unscrewed the cap with a starved fervor, bolting down its contents in three huge gulps. Her cap fell off with her eagerness, landing between their feet.

"Alright," Honey said. "Hot."

"Shut up," Sadie mumbled against the thermos.

Blood spilled down her chin. She resurfaced with a shudder, her eyes black. "Ugh. That's *so* gross."

"And yet you keep eating it. Animals: truly the pop tarts of blood."

"Pop tarts are *good*, you're just weird." Sadie uncapped another thermos and sucked that down just as fast as the first.

Before she could reach for the third, Honey's phone rang.

Honey dug it out. *Caller unknown.*

Sadie stared at it. A drop of blood hung at the end of her chin, ready to break off.

Honey darted forward to lick it clean.

"Hello," she slurred into the phone, grinning at Sadie's swollen pupils.

"Hiiii," trilled a familiar perky voice. "Is this Honey Williams?"

Honey hummed, smacking blood between her lips. "Let me guess. Spookytimegirlies04?"

"Oh my god, that's so weird. And cool! I hope I haven't freaked you out with my videos. How are you?"

Honey looked around Sadie's messy room. Curtains drawn, two empty thermoses of blood on the bed, one of them full and waiting. Munson out the front scrubbing eggs off the front door. A secret girlfriend in front of her, eyes completely black except for a speck of gold in the middle, watching Honey's mouth hungrily.

Honey's tongue flicked out, cleaning a drop of blood from her lip. Sadie blinked hard, looking disappointed.

*It blocks everything else out*, Sadie had told her, white-knuckling the steering wheel. *I can't think about anything but how hungry I am.*

"I'm awesome," Honey said flatly.

"Great! I was wondering if you wanted to get coffee? I'm buying."

Honey hummed for a long time, gearing up to tell Clarissa every way she could fuck off. Then she noticed Sadie's thoughtful expression.

Honey covered the speaker. "What?"

Sadie hesitated. "I say we do it."

Honey waited. When Sadie didn't continue, Honey ventured cautiously: "Like...kill her?"

"Jesus! No! *Meet* her, *talk* to her."

"Oooooh, a little threaty-threat." Honey shimmied her hips. "I love your twisted mind."

Sadie caught her wrist before she could uncover the phone. "*Or* we give her a false lead. Say we saw the bassist heading into that bathroom with an ax, or something. And we didn't want to say anything because everyone was being so weird about it all."

Honey hummed some more. On the phone, Clarissa was repeating, "Um, hello? Helloooo?"

"Spooky girl," Honey said. "You want to talk? Let's talk. I'll drop you a pin with my location."

"Oh! Okay, I—"

Honey hung up and reached for the last thermos on the bed.

Sadie started, "Where are we..."

She fell silent as Honey uncapped the remaining thermos, tilting it to reveal the dark liquid inside.

"Drink your possum blood," she instructed.

Sadie's nostrils flared. "Aw," she said, distracted. "I love possums."

"Possums are freaky looking."

"Not in New Zealand," Sadie said, and tipped the thermos into her mouth. Honey watched her throat work, the bob of her throat fast and constant, not slowing down until it was empty.

"Well," she said as Sadie resurfaced. "We're not in New Zealand."

Sadie ran her tongue around the red rim. "You don't want any?"

"I'm fine." Honey smiled reassuringly. "And you will be, in another week or two. How's the head?"

Sadie twisted her head. The horrifying hole in her skull was gone, replaced by a thick sheen of black hair. Honey felt the scalp underneath. Cool and intact.

"Battle-ready," Honey said. "Let's go lie our asses off."

It was getting dark. Not that it mattered to creatures like them.

Honey squinted through the trees, trying to identify a crawling thing on a branch. When she was a child she used to walk through these same woods with an encyclopedia, dragging her mom and Sadie around to identify spiders and beetles and butterflies. The woods looked smaller than when she was a kid, and yet infinitely bigger. She could see the veins of faraway leaves. See the individual hairs on an ant's leg. Smell critters digging holes or curling up under bushes. The woods were so much more alive now she was dead.

She nudged Sadie. "How does that poem go? *The woods are hungry, dark and deep...*"

"*The woods are* lovely, *dark and deep*," Sadie corrected. She frowned. "*Something, something, miles, sleep.*"

"Huh." Honey stretched her neck, feeling the joints pop. "I like my version better."

Footsteps. Faint cursing, a foot catching on a root. Honey sucked in a breath: sweat, cinnamon, coffee, ice, sugar.

Clarissa burst through the trees. Her glasses were crooked, one sleeve of her blazer stained with moss. She wobbled on her ankle boots, clutching a huge Starbucks cup in each hand.

"Oh my god," she said as she noticed them. "I thought I was lost!"

"Nope," Honey said. "Right where you're meant to be."

Clarissa held out the Starbucks cups. "This is for you!"

"We're not huge fans of iced drinks," Sadie said.

"Really not," Honey agreed, looking sadly at the cups. They were topped with whipped cream and caramel drizzle. Her kind of drink, once upon a time. Sadie's, too, unless Sadie had pretended to be that "black coffee with no sugar" type of teen, which was entirely possible.

"Oh. Oookay." Clarissa sipped one of the straws. Then the other. "I thought you two didn't hang out? That's what Sadie said when I talked to her, like, two hours ago?"

"We don't," Honey said.

"I lied," Sadie said over her. She went to glance at Honey, then stopped herself. *The less eye contact the better*, Honey had told her while they waited for Clarissa to show up. *I know it's hard to tear your eyes off of my bodacious bod—*

*I didn't look at you for years*, Sadie had said waspishly. *I can manage it.*

"This is stupid," Sadie said. "Somebody egged my house tonight. Everybody was *really* weird at school, and...look, we *don't* hang out. Seriously. The road trip was some stupid bucket list thing, same as being an opener for a band. We snuck into that bar, lied our way onstage, ran off when the bouncer came to get us. We didn't kill anyone! But—"

"We saw something," Honey said. "While we were running."

Clarissa's eyes were wide behind her useless glasses. "What?"

"The bassist," Sadie said. "He was heading for the bathroom. The bathroom it all happened in."

"Was he holding anything?"

"An ax," Sadie said.

"I don't know," Honey said over her.

They glared at each other. They'd had this argument while they were waiting—was it too convenient?—and Honey had *thought* they'd come to a conclusion.

"We didn't get a great look," Honey tried. "It *could've* been an ax."

"We weren't paying much attention," Sadie added. "With all the running."

Clarissa nodded, digging in her pocket. "Would you be willing to say that on camera?"

"No," Honey and Sadie said as one, loud enough to startle birds from trees.

Sadie grimaced and continued, "*Actually* we were hoping you would say you found that witness somewhere else. And you could say we weren't actually there. Because if you say we *were* there, our classmates are going to get even weirder, and I refuse to put up with that crap for the rest of the year."

"Mysterious band didn't do anything, they just saw some stuff, and they have nothing to do with two ex-besties in Tennessee. Tell *that* to your YouTube followers," Honey said, and frowned. "Followers? *Subscribers*. Let *that* one go viral. Not a video about two girls in the armpit of America pretending to be a band one time."

Clarissa laughed nervously. "It didn't actually go viral. It reached 80k! That's...yes, that's a lot more than my usual videos, but that's not viral *yet*." She bit her lip. "What about the man who got attacked last night?"

"I really was home," Sadie said.

"Me too," Honey said. "Painting my nails."

It was even true. They didn't have to tell her that she did it while Sadie lay in the bathtub healing from a hole in the head and drinking animal blood.

"And even if we weren't," Honey continued. "That's my friend's dad, she showed me photos. *No* human is able to do that to another human."

Clarissa shifted from foot to foot, obviously uncomfortable. The cinnamon was almost gone now, drowned out by sweat.

"I really think you should say that on the record," she said, and giggled. "On the record, like I'm a cop. No, like... you should say it, or let me say it, or I'll *call* the cops."

"For what?" Honey cleared her throat. Her voice had gone way too shrill. "We didn't do anything!"

"Noooo..." Clarissa honest-to-god twirled her hair, still deeply uncomfortable, still one hundred percent going for it. "I just think they'd wanna talk to the last two people who saw the wanted murder suspect."

Honey stared at her. "Wait. Are you...are *you* threatening *us*?"

"No!" Clarissa stopped, considering. "I mean... maybe?"

Honey turned to stare at Sadie, who had rejected her threat idea so quickly, but Sadie wasn't looking at her.

She wasn't even looking at Clarissa. Her head was cocked, eyes tracking the trees. Listening.

Honey whispered, "What?"

Sadie's head cocked further. "Someone's here. Listen."

Honey focused. Bugs in the dirt. An animal snuffling for food. Then, finally, a dozen yards away: tobacco. Leather. The slow, even sound of somebody breathing. A soft clicking noise Honey couldn't identify, something sliding into place.

Clarissa whispered, "I don't hear—"

An arrow streaked into the clearing and embedded itself in her calf.

chapter
## six

CLARISSA SHRIEKED. Her drinks plummeted to the ground, splashing iced coffee all over her bleeding leg. Her glasses fell, the plastic lenses cracking.

"OH MY GOD," she screamed, folding over in agony. "WHAT THE HECK? OW, OH MY GOD, OW!"

Honey shuddered as the thick scent of blood filled the clearing. She scrabbled for her humanity, reaching for anything that wasn't the hunger tearing up her insides. What she came to was this: later, she would turn to Sadie and ask, *who gets shot and says heck?*

But not right now. Sadie stood predator-still, her lips peeling back from her sharpening teeth.

Underneath Clarissa's screaming, there was a low click of a crossbow reloading.

Sadie crouched, ready to pounce.

"Nope," Honey blurted, and tackled her.

A second arrow whistled over their heads. Honey shoved Sadie into the ground, an arm across her neck.

"Stay," she growled.

Sadie snapped at her, teeth grazing Honey's forearm.

"We have bigger shit to deal with right now," Honey said, and looked up.

Clarissa was on one knee, clutching her bleeding calf. Iced coffee leaked into her shoes as she stared, horrified, at Sadie's writhing form.

"This is fine," Honey assured her weakly. She held her breath, thinking back to Mr. Lu. Knowing she was the only thing between Sadie and an innocent person getting murdered. Kind of wanting it to happen anyway, just so she could have a taste of their blood before Sadie drained it.

Another low click. Honey turned toward it just in time for the man to step through the trees, crossbow aloft.

A leather coat hung to his ankles. His boots were leather, his belt snakeskin with a metal snake's head for a buckle. He had a cowboy hat. He had a *toothpick*, and he was chewing it distractedly as he aimed at Honey.

If Honey was even a little less scared, she would have giggled.

"Nope," she squeaked again, and rolled them over.

The next arrow thudded into the grass where Honey's torso had been. Sadie yowled, clawing at Honey's back as they rolled over and over until Honey had her pinned once more to the ground.

"Shut up, I'm *helping*," Honey yelled, arm back on Sadie's throat.

She looked over. The man was advancing. He drew closer as Clarissa retreated, dragging herself toward the tree line and fumbling for something in her pocket.

Honey turned back to her thrashing, feral girlfriend. Then at the man who definitely watched *Van Helsing* too many times. He raised the crossbow again.

"We can take you," Honey yelled, adrenaline making her voice shake. "Two of us against one of you? We'll get hurt, but we'll make it. You? You'll be our new chew toy."

The man paused.

"You want that?" Honey sat up, feigning like she was going to let Sadie go. Sadie reared up, teeth snapping toward the man's legs.

The man stared down at them. His mouth twisted around his toothpick, and he swung the crossbow around until it was pointing straight at Clarissa.

Clarissa made a noise like a dying bird. She had her phone out, camera pointed at the scene unfolding in front of her.

"Really," Honey asked. "Now?"

Clarissa didn't respond. Her fingers were white and trembling around the phone, a tear dripping down her face.

"You better not be livestreaming this," Honey said.

Clarissa let out a pained whimper, eyes locked on the crossbow pointing at her head.

"You should've kept your nose out of things you don't understand," the man said. His voice was less gravelly than Honey had expected. "Now look where you ended up. Leverage for a vampire hunter."

"Oh my god," Honey said. "Get *over* yourself."

"Shut up," he jeered. His toothpick shifted to the other side of his mouth. "You two come with me. Come *quietly*. Or the girl dies."

Honey's brain shorted out. She was sure she should know more about hostage situations. They'd done a whole assembly about it in second grade, and for years after Sadie had been convinced one of them would get kidnapped.

She was pretty sure the main rule was: don't let the guy take you to a second location. Did this count as the first location, or was this location zero?

Before Honey could make a decision, Sadie's arm squirmed free. Her fist whipped into Honey's head so hard and fast that Honey fell to the side.

Sadie rose in a blur. The man swore, crossbow swinging around toward the charging vampire. An arrow lodged in Sadie's elbow.

Too late. Sadie was on him, yowling, her gnashing teeth only stopped by the man shoving the crossbow in between them. His cowboy hat lay beside him, knocked off in the tussle.

Honey lurched over to them, locking her arms around Sadie's neck and pulling.

"Let us go or I let her kill you right now," Honey said.

Sadie didn't acknowledge the bolt in her elbow or the grip around her neck. She was too busy biting the crossbow, trying to chew through it. Trying to get to the skin underneath.

Fear flashed through the man's eyes. Honey was tempted to let Sadie kill him no matter what. He *shot* her. Would've shot Honey, if she didn't roll out of the way. But Clarissa was still pointing that phone at them, and Honey had no idea if this was live or not. Rumors were bad enough. Footage of Honey letting her girlfriend eat someone was pretty damning. Even Honey Williams, popular hottie and upcoming prom queen, couldn't recover from that.

Sadie strained harder. The crossbow dented under her fangs.

"Well?" Honey asked. "What's it gonna be, asshole?"

The man glared. He bit through his toothpick, spitting it into the dirt.

"Get her off of me," he demanded.

Honey yanked. It took all her strength to pull Sadie up enough for the man to scrabble out from underneath her, grabbing his cowboy hat. For a moment the man just stood there, and Honey thought they'd have to kill him after all. Then his gaze darted to the side, where Clarissa was filming with shaking hands.

"This isn't over," he said darkly. Then he strode off into the woods, leather coat billowing behind him.

"Asshole," Honey called after him.

Sadie bucked in her arms, still snarling.

Honey shook her. "Shut up, you needy little bitch."

Clarissa let out a sob. Her mouth quivered. Her leg was bleeding freely. Honey hadn't noticed her pull the arrow out, but it was lying in a sticky puddle with the iced coffees.

Honey sighed and pressed her mouth next to Sadie's ear, trying to remember what she said to bring Sadie back after attacking Mr. Lu.

"Hey," she whispered. "You gotta come back now. Hear me? Come back to me. Just look at me, quit looking at her leg, look at me. I'm so much hotter than a leg wound, come on, turn your head and—yeah, that's it."

Sadie blinked. Some of the black seeped out of her eyes, replaced by that blazing green.

"Hon...ey," she said, slurring around her fangs. Like she only half remembered how to speak.

Honey blew out a relieved breath. "You back now? Good. Oh my god, you're such a *handful*. If I go over and heal Clarissa, are you gonna try and bite her?"

Sadie paused. Her eyes flickered.

"It'll make it easier," Honey promised, and carefully let her go. Sadie twitched, but didn't move from her spot as Honey went to Clarissa.

Clarissa crawled back, phone still in front of her. "What are you doing?"

"Healing you," Honey said. "Weren't you listening? Hold still."

She bent down and sunk her fangs around Clarissa's wound. Clarissa shrieked, moving her phone like she wanted to smack Honey with it, but averted her aim at the last moment.

Honey concentrated. She didn't suck, despite the sweet blood dripping into her mouth. The soft buzzing filled her jaw as she pushed venom into the wound, making Clarissa gasp in shocked pleasure. Her phone fell into her lap, fingers slack and useless.

Honey pulled back and licked the wound. More spit. More venom. The jagged hole was already starting to close up.

She looked back at Sadie. "Better?"

Sadie didn't reply. She was staring at the arrow in her elbow, face creasing as the pain finally set in.

"Ow," she said. "*Shit.*"

Clarissa made another noise. The venom was starting to fade. She shuddered, the dazed rapture leaving her expression.

She grabbed her phone out of her lap.

"T-tell me what the heck is going on," she croaked. "Or I post this right now!"

Honey considered. Then she grabbed the phone and threw it against a tree. Plastic and metal shattered all over the clearing.

Clarissa let out another sob. "I saved it to my drafts! I can just log in on my laptop!"

Honey groaned. She looked back at Sadie to see if she had any idea what to do next, only to see Sadie yanking the arrow out of her arm with a pained hiss.

"Ew." Honey grimaced and turned back to Clarissa. "Whatever. Come with us."

"Are you going to kill me?"

Honey blinked as the stupidity of that comment sunk in.

"If we were going to kill you," she said slowly, "we would have let him shoot you. Or let Sadie eat you. That's twice I've saved your life, you no-talent pathetic excuse for an influencer! You're welcome!"

Clarissa sniffed. Her lip wobbled. "What *are* you?"

Honey rolled her eyes. "We're—"

Sadie cut her off, lips pinched. Making sure she didn't inhale. "Come with us," she said, strained. "And we'll tell you."

Clarissa stared up at them with wide, tear-filled eyes. She twisted to see the hole in her leg. Her mouth fell open as she watched the bloody skin knit itself together.

Honey held out her hand.

Clarissa sniffed and took it.

*Ashes to ashes,* Honey thought as Sadie lay bleeding in her own bathtub. *Bathrooms to bathrooms.*

She asked, "Is *ashes to ashes, bathrooms to bathrooms* a good song lyric?"

Sadie stared at her. So did Clarissa, curled up on top

of the closed toilet lid. She'd started hugging her knees before Honey had even finished telling her about waking up dead in the woods—omitting the dead cop beside her, of course—and hadn't stopped now that the story was finished.

"Maybe leave the songwriting to me," Sadie told her. She winced, injured arm sliding against the porcelain. Black blood oozed into the bottom of the tub.

Clarissa pressed her hand over the healed skin of her calf. "Can you go out in the sunlight?"

"We went to school today," Honey replied.

"Oh," Clarissa said weakly. "That's...good. School is good."

She stared at the ugly bathroom wallpaper, not seeing any of it. Honey turned to give Sadie a pointed look, but Sadie's eyes were shut tight. Focusing on anything but Clarissa's beating heart on the other side of the room.

"I'm so sorry," Clarissa burst, pressing her face into her knees. "I never meant for this to happen! Everybody's like, careful what you put up on the internet, weirdos can find you, and I was always like, sure, whatever! You know? And everyone loves this story! On the way back here I finally got a notification that YouTube's gonna start paying me! Not a lot, but it means I won't have to go back and work for that hot dog hut—"

Honey cut her off. "We need to find out who he is."

"Your sire," Sadie asked, eyes still shut. "Or the guy who shot me?"

"The guy who shot you!"

Clarissa wiped her wet cheeks. "I have footage of his face. I can put a screenshot up."

"And say he shot us?"

"No! I'll just say he's potentially related to the case." Clarissa's nails dug into her intact, bloody calf. "And that he's dangerous."

*You should've kept your nose out of things you don't understand*, he'd told Clarissa.

Honey sighed. "He watches your videos. He'll know you're onto him."

Clarissa turned her wide, wet eyes on them. "You guys will protect me, right?"

Honey looked over at Sadie. Sadie's eyes were still closed, head back against the lip of the bathtub.

"Also," Clarissa added. "Can I stay at someone's house tonight? I thought this was just a day trip."

Honey tapped Sadie on the shoulder. When Sadie opened her eyes, Honey was holding a closed fist in front of her face.

"Rock, paper, scissors," Honey said flatly. "Go."

# seven

"VAMPIRE HUNTERS," Milly Hart repeated over speakerphone. "Why?"

"Just curious. One second." Sadie dropped a handful of wet mulch off the roof. "Incoming!"

Clarissa held a tarp wide. The mulch hit the growing pile with a wet *thwack*.

Clarissa whooped, wobbling under the weight. "We're doing so good!"

"Uh-huh, doing great." Sadie wrinkled her nose at the mulch left to clean out of the gutters. Vampire pros: super speed, super strength, limited amount of flight. Vampire cons: almost everything else. A hyper sense of smell *sucked*. Especially in her house, which hadn't been cleaned since Sadie was prepubescent.

"They're definitely around," Milly said, her voice floating out from the phone Sadie had stuck in a clean bit of gutter. "They generally don't bother vampires who aren't...you know."

"Going around killing people," Sadie supplied.

"As far as I know," Milly continued.

Clarissa held the tarp out wider, stage whispering: "Who is this lady again?"

"She owns a bookshop," Sadie told her. "She blessed Honey's guitar and she's the closest thing we have to information about any of this vampire crap."

"Oh," Clarissa said, blinking owlishly. "O...kay."

Milly sighed. "I'm sorry I can't be more help. There isn't...a *network* for this. We find who we can find and listen to what they have to say. Then we go off of that until someone else shows up and tells us different."

"Awesome. Fills me with hope." Sadie scooped another handful of mulch out of the gutter and tried not to gag. Rot was bad enough when she was human. Now she could taste it, thick and cloying in the back of her throat. She'd have to shower twice after this, coating herself in peach body soap until she smelled like sweet fake fruit instead of death and decay. She dropped the wet handful and watched it splat into Clarissa's tarp.

"The vampire hunters I've met have been nice enough," Milly said. "It's the families you have to watch out for."

"Families?"

"Passing it down the generations. They can get very, uh, passionate about it." Milly hissed. "Ow! Paper cut. Anyway, how are you doing?"

Sadie paused, shoving the last of the mulch out of the

gutter. "Fine. I mean good. We're good. Nothing happened."

Clarissa shot her a grimy thumbs-up. Sadie ignored her, crawling over to her phone and plucking it out from the cleaned gutter.

"Alright," Milly said slowly. "Well. I'm here if you need anything. Like another blessing, or a translation. I can't fight. Please don't call if you need a fighter."

"Can Frankie and Ivy fight?" Sadie asked, only half-joking. At Clarissa's confused look, she clarified: "They're lesbians in New York. Also involved in vampire stuff."

"As much as any average person on the street," Milly replied. "So, no. And Frankie and Ivy were never involved in vampire stuff directly, they had their own stuff going on. Do you need—"

Down on the lawn, Clarissa squeaked. Sadie's dad was leaning out from underneath the front porch, face slack with sleep.

"We're fine thanks bye," Sadie mumbled, ending the call.

Munson blinked blearily. First at Sadie, then at Clarissa sheepishly holding a tarp full of gutter mulch.

"Kid," Munson croaked. He cleared his throat. "The hell you doing?"

Sadie shoved her phone into her sweatpants pocket and stood, balancing perfectly on the tiles, no human clumsiness holding her back. "What does it look like?"

"Looks like it's seven a.m."

Sadie shrugged. "Couldn't sleep."

She bent down, then froze. There was no ladder. She couldn't scale the drainpipe or float down like she'd been planning. Not with her dad watching.

It was so much worse without Honey at her side. Nights on the drive back had been *fun*, Honey in the passenger's seat or lounging next to Sadie in a motel bed they didn't actually need. They had stopped at the side of the road to sniff out wild animals to feed on. Made out without stopping for breath, watched *Gilmore Girls* and argued over which characters they were supposed to like. Honey spent twenty minutes talking about a bedbug she'd plucked from their motel mattress and Sadie had found herself thinking, *this is the most fun I've had since middle school.*

But last night wasn't *fun*. Last night was everything Sadie feared about being a vampire: lying stiff on the carpet (Clarissa took the bed), listening to loud music through her headphones and waiting for the hours to pass. How many times had she done this during a sleepless night? The only difference was she had to stop herself from ripping into the nearest warm body.

Munson squinted up at her, still only half-awake. "So you dragged your friend out here to clean the gutters?"

Sadie crawled to the edge of the roof and slung her legs over, ignoring Munson's wary look. "Have you noticed how gross our house is, Dad? Like, EVERY-THING smells like dust. Or mold. There's definitely something rotting in the cupboard, we're gonna get mice again."

*Good*, said an imaginary Honey. *You can eat the mice.*

Clarissa heaved the tarp to the ground, both hands locked around the ends to stop the mulch from spilling out over the lawn. "Good morning, Mr. Greer! Thank you again for letting me stay, it's so nice of you."

"No problem," Munson said, with the confused air of a man who didn't get called *nice* very often. "Remind me how you know my daughter?"

"Internet friends," the two of them chorused.

Munson rubbed his stubbly chin. "Uh-huh. Which website?"

Sadie paused.

"Tumblr," Clarissa said hastily, her smile far too wide for seven a.m. "We drifted apart a few years ago, though. Which is why you didn't hear about me. Yay for friends reconnecting!"

Munson blinked at her with that same bewildered expression he always got when people got too smiley for no reason. *I feel like they're trying to sell me a toaster*, he liked to tell Sadie afterward. He tolerated it from Honey, but grudgingly.

The silence stretched. Clarissa opened her mouth awkwardly.

Munson cut her off. "You like coffee?"

Clarissa beamed. "I *love* coffee!"

He looked up at Sadie.

"No," Sadie said. Then, as an afterthought: "Thank you."

Munson nodded and headed back inside. Sadie listened to the door close and sagged in relief, thanking fate that her dad was too tired to realize there was no ladder for her to climb down. She stood up again, not bothering to step carefully as she headed for the drainpipe.

"Wait," Clarissa said, dumping the tarp next to the porch steps. "You said you could fly, right?"

Sadie sighed. "Fine, but make sure he doesn't come out again."

She paused. Then she stepped off the roof.

Clarissa squeaked in excitement.

"Don't," Sadie said, concentrating. It was less of a fly and more of a concentrated hover, and it felt...*tight*. Like the cabin being pressurized in an airplane. The closer she got to the ground, the looser her head felt. By the time her bare feet touched the grass, the pressure in her head was gone and Clarissa was jumping up and down.

"Show's over," Sadie said. "Quit it. I gotta get ready for school."

Clarissa stopped jumping, digging her teeth into her lower lip to stop herself from grinning. It didn't work. Her heartbeat was up, her cheeks flushed.

"Quit it," Sadie said again.

"Quit what?"

Sadie ignored her, heading up the porch steps.

Clarissa followed. "So you and Honey are gonna

pretend you're not friends," she whispered when they reached Sadie's room.

"I guess." Sadie pulled her drawers open, sifting through her clothes. Flannel. Tank tops. Hoodies. Sometimes she loved her old clothes. Other times they felt like a cocoon she couldn't escape.

"That's rough," Clarissa said, perching on the end of Sadie's mattress. She'd made the bed after she woke up, straightening the duvet with a fervor that suggested she didn't make her own bed very much and was only semi-sure of how it went.

"Do your friends know?"

Sadie hesitated. "Honey's don't."

"And yours?"

Sadie slammed the drawer shut. "What are you doing all day?"

Clarissa made a face. "Doomscroll? Reply to comments? There isn't anything useful about our guy yet, but I'm sure we'll find something."

"Yeah? What do your friends think about you randomly taking off?"

Clarissa laughed nervously, pulling at her sleeves. "Um, most of them went to college out of state. Anyway, have a good day at school! Don't eat anyone."

"No promises," Sadie said darkly.

Sadie kept her head down. Ignored all the whispers. Put on her headphones in the halls between classes. She was still wearing headphones as she hunched over her cafeteria tray, eyes closed, trying to focus on the apple she couldn't eat instead of all the warm bodies filling the room with their flimsy skin and pulsing blood—

A whisper broke through the blaring music. Sadie frowned.

*Sadie*. It sounded like Honey. So quiet, and yet still breaking through the din.

She opened her eyes.

Honey was at her usual table, sandwiched between Summer and Britney. Her hand was up over her mouth, covering her whisper, and her expression was so pissed off she couldn't even look at the person causing it: Ken leaned against the table with a cocksure grin, an acoustic guitar in his hands.

Sadie took her headphones off.

"Haven't heard you sing for ages," Ken was saying. "Terms and conditions changed. We need an audition before you get up to sing in front of everybody at my party."

"You heard me sing last year," Honey said waspishly, twisting her pigtails hard around her fingers. "You heard me sing last *month*."

"Really? Huh. I don't remember that." Ken turned to the rest of the cafeteria, hoisting the guitar in the air. "Who wants to hear Honey Williams's golden pipes?"

The cafeteria burst into cheers and whoops. For a moment it drowned out the constant thud of heartbeats in Sadie's ears.

"Come on," Ken goaded. "Practice for when you're a superstar."

Honey's jaw flexed. She whipped around, fixing him with a withering look. "I haven't wanted to be a singer since ninth grade."

"Come on!" Ken spread his arms, gesturing for the cheering to start up again. A few people gave him half-hearted whoops. "Everybody wants to be a star. You're telling me Honey Williams wouldn't eat that shit up?"

"For an hour, sure," Honey snapped. "But being on tour would *suck*. Being a rock star is a stupid pipe dream for kids!"

Something crunched. Sadie looked down to find she'd clenched the cafeteria table so hard the plastic had cracked. She closed her eyes, thinking about anything but the howling hunger and Honey at ten years old, telling Sadie being in a band with her was the only thing she ever wanted.

"Ken, just shut *up*," Summer said as Sadie fumbled, eyes closed, for her headphones. "This isn't funny anymore, people should be looking for that scumbag bassist who *obviously* did it but instead everybody's posting memes about your ex—"

Sadie shoved her headphones back on. Music blared through her head, taking over from the deafening thud of heartbeats. She didn't dare breathe, but the scent of ripe skin washed in anyway. Maybe she would skip last period and go hunting. Screw Honey and her worry, Sadie would just be super careful. Make sure there were no people for miles before she went feral on some poor raccoon.

Another whisper, even softer than the last. All this noise and Honey's voice still cut her to the bone.

*Sadie.*

Her eyes flew open just in time to watch Ken Lu sling an acoustic guitar on the table, narrowly missing her tray.

"—want her there," Ken finished saying as Sadie yanked her headphones off. He was looking toward Honey's table. For a second Sadie thought he was taunting Honey again, but then she saw him wink in Britney's direction.

Britney winked back. Honey whipped around to look at her, and Britney pretended to have something stuck in her eye.

Ken turned to Sadie and grinned, curling his tongue over his teeth like an asshole. "What do you say, Greer? Wanna make a hundred bucks?"

Sadie stiffened and hated herself for it. Ken loomed over her with that cocky smile, and Sadie was frozen. Like she couldn't rip him apart with her bare hands. Like she couldn't take down everyone who was staring right now, a good third of the cafeteria watching the show.

"No," Sadie said brusquely. She picked up an apple from her tray, digging her fingers into the skin.

"You haven't even heard what I want yet! Here's the deal." Ken leaned in, snapping his puka shell necklace against his collarbones. "You and Honey play at my birthday party. Sounds fun, right? Except I haven't heard you play since middle school, so you gotta audition for me."

He pushed the guitar further up the table, making her tray slide dangerously close to the edge.

Summer piped up from her table, meatloaf dangling off her fork. "Ken, this stopped being funny yesterday. Quit being a dick."

Ken flipped her off without looking back. His eager gaze was fixed purely on Sadie, like he'd learned that staring into a dog's eyes asserted dominance.

*Wrong*, Sadie thought. *It's a threat.*

"Come on," Ken goaded. He plucked the sleeve of her flannel shirt, too close to the bandage. "Clothes you wear, you gotta be hurting for money. One hundred bucks."

Honey's chair screeched as she stood. "Alright, I'm outta here. Later, shitbirds."

*Don't go,* Sadie thought. The thought stung. It felt young and huge and stupid.

Ken's smile flickered as he watched Honey march out with Summer and Britney on her heels.

Sadie's fingers tightened around the apple. Honey had left again. Ken was leaning so close, his heartbeat steady under that stupid necklace. It would be so *easy* to grab his big hair and drag him in.

He snapped his fingers in front of her face. "Hey! Are you paying attention? I'm making a business proposition here."

Sadie's thumbnail dug into the apple flesh, straight to the core.

Ken leaned in further. Deodorant wafted from his skin. Not enough to hide the heady scent of skin underneath, heady and *waiting*.

"You can't tell me you don't want a reunion tour," Ken whispered.

Sadie wanted to say something cool. *I wouldn't play for you for a million bucks.* But she could feel her teeth growing sharp in her mouth.

She closed her eyes again. Her eyes were flickering black. She could feel her pupils swell.

"Hey," Ken said. "Are you—is she seriously closing her eyes right now?"

He waved a hand in front of her face. His heartbeat pounded in his wrist. A luscious river ran through his arm, right underneath the thin skin.

Sadie's fangs pricked her tongue. She was so *hungry*.

Ken leaned in even further. His heartbeat was so loud Sadie barely heard him say, "Hey. I'm *talking* to—"

A shrill shriek cut the world in half.

Ken swore, leaping back.

Sadie sat very still. The noise was earsplitting and horrible and for a moment she thought it was coming from her. Then she opened her eyes and saw everybody was grabbing their backpacks and heading, groaning, toward the cafeteria door as the fire alarm continued to shriek.

Sadie blinked. Honey was leaning on the doorway,

texting with a bored expression. The triggered fire alarm was directly behind her.

Sadie's phone vibrated. She dug it out of her pocket. Two unseen messages.

The first one read:

*ur welcome <3*

The second was from Clarissa. A link to a Facebook profile, and underneath it:

*bingo bitches!!!*

# chapter
## eight

HONEY WALKED to the playground alone.

*Their* playground. The playground where they'd made the blood vow when they were kids, right in the middle of an empty park. She rounded the corner to see two girls sitting in the swings and got smacked violently with déjà vu: that was Sadie, the same sharp face and big eyes. But the other girl was wrong.

"Out," Honey told Clarissa as she strode up.

Clarissa paused mid-sip of her iced coffee, a laptop balanced in her lap. "Huh?"

Honey sighed, tugging with irritation on one of her pigtails. "That's my swing. Get out."

"Okay," Clarissa chirped, instead of the sensible answer, which was *get your own swing, jackass.* Honey looked at Sadie, expecting that answer written in her eye roll. But Sadie was staring at nothing, eyes glazed, a muscle flexing in her jaw. She didn't even glance at Honey sliding into the swing next to Sadie, the swings that used to be so high their feet hung above the ground when they sat down.

They'd reached across this very space, blood dripping down their pinkies.

*To death and beyond.*

"I was just telling Sadie his name is Elijah," Clarissa said, balancing the iced coffee on the open laptop she was holding. "One of my followers linked me his Facebook."

She chewed anxiously at the straw of her drink, glancing around the empty park. She was still wearing the useless glasses. The lenses were more obviously plastic the longer Honey looked at them.

"Are we safe out here? Like, even minus the hunter, you guys can't be seen together, right?"

Honey pulled at the rusty swing chain. "This park has been unofficially closed for business for years. Nobody comes here unless they're dealing drugs, doing drugs, or having sex inside the slide."

Clarissa frowned at the slide, which had a sizable hole in the roof. "It's...a little small."

Honey snorted. "Yeah, last year Britney got stuck under Sam Ferris."

Sadie blinked, her gaze coming back into focus. "Sam *Ferris*?"

Honey took it and ran with it. "Right? Get some *standards*, Brit."

"Says the girl who dated Ken Lu."

"He's hot!"

"And an asshole."

"And *hot*," Honey repeated.

Sadie scoffed. "Glad to know what *your* standards are."

Honey winked. She was so caught up in the joy of coaxing annoying, sharp, *fun* Sadie out of strained, hungry, *boring* Sadie that she didn't notice Clarissa staring awkwardly at them until she cleared her throat.

"Ugh," Honey said. "Right. Guy trying to kill us is called Elijah."

Clarissa nodded, holding up her hand to reveal a bunch of smudged notes. "Elijah Harkner, midfifties, not married, no kids. He's from Arkansas. My source says he's a total loner and he travels out of state a lot for 'work.' He's a drinker, a Leo, and he once cut off my source's mom in a drugstore parking lot and then *he* flipped *her* off."

"Aw," Honey drawled. "The guy who tried to murder us is rude, Sadie."

Clarissa ignored them, scrolling one-handed. "Lots of people are saying I'm making it up? People are even saying The Bleeding Bastards are fake and everyone who says they watched them IRL is lying. Or an actor."

She ducked her head to sip at her iced coffee. It wobbled on her laptop, and Honey's mouth twitched as she imagined it spilling over the keyboard.

"We're good," Clarissa squeaked, standing very still so she didn't jostle her drink or laptop. "That was so close. I just got my car fixed, I can*not* afford..."

Sadie stiffened. Honey tuned out whatever Clarissa was blathering about to turn to her.

"What? If you're about to hulk out on Clarissa, I will wrap this swing chain around your neck."

Sadie shot to her feet. "Someone's coming. Two people and a dog."

"Come *on*," Honey whined. She strained, and there it was: two voices coming around the corner, a dog panting below them.

"Oh my god," Clarissa blurted, grabbing her iced coffee in one hand, pushing the laptop closed with her chin. "What do we *do*?"

Honey turned to Sadie. "Hide! Go! Go, go, go!" She slapped Sadie's arms like she'd seen the coach do to football players before big games.

"Fine, but you're hiding next time," Sadie spat. She blurred toward the slide and leapt in just in time for a middle-aged couple to round the corner, a tiny spaniel yanking on the leash ahead of them.

Honey gritted her teeth in a smile. She knew that dog, and she knew that couple.

The newly empty swing swayed. Clarissa paced in front of it, squeezing her laptop to her chest, her plastic cup denting around her fingers. "This is cool. We're cool. We're just two gals, hanging at the park! Having a chat. Honey, why are you *staring*?"

"Because they're waving," Honey told her through a gritted smile. She raised her hand to wave back at them. "Hi, Mr. and Mrs. Lu!"

Clarissa gasped. Honey couldn't tell if she recognized the name or saw the man's wounds and put two and two together.

Mr. Lu's shoulder was swathed in white, bandages peeking out from his loose-fitting shirt. There was another bandage on his forehead. Honey didn't remember Sadie biting his forehead. It must have happened when Sadie knocked him to the ground. His hands were dotted with tiny healing cuts from twigs and stones catching on his skin as he flailed.

Honey swallowed the spit pooling in her mouth and glanced at the slide. No signs of movement. This was good. It meant Sadie wasn't ready to lunge.

Honey forced a giggle. "The man, the myth, the bear-fighting legend! Looking good, Mr. Lu."

Mr. Lu chuckled in that confused way he did when he wasn't sure whether Honey was insulting him. He looked uncomfortable and sweaty, but there was no suspicion in his gaze. He didn't recognize her from those dark woods.

"There was no fighting, Honey. But thank you."

His wife rubbed his good shoulder. "He's looking great, isn't he? The doctors said to avoid strenuous exercise, but I think this is fine."

Mr. Lu nodded. Sweat beaded at his hairline, dripping into the bandage.

The dog barked and flashed its tiny teeth at Honey.

Mrs. Lu frowned, tugging the leash. "Buster, calm down, it's just Honey! Honestly, this dog."

Honey bent down to coo at him. "Hi, Buster!"

Buster growled, backing away.

Honey stood back up with a wince. Buster had *loved* her last month.

"Ooookay then. Well, I'll let you get back to your walk."

"Oh, we can spare a moment. Let Ben get his breath back." Mrs. Lu glanced at Clarissa curiously. "Hi there! I don't think we've met. Are you coming to my son's birthday party? It feels like every teenager I run into is suddenly on the guest list, and I need to know the *proper* numbers for the catering. You understand."

A whisper drifted over from the slide, inaudible to human ears. *"Go away!"*

Honey bit her cheek, imagining Sadie folding herself into a tiny ball in that stupid broken slide. "She's out of town by then. BTW, your earrings are *so* hot, Mrs. Lu."

"Oh, these old things?" Mrs. Lu thumbed the elegant hoops dangling from her ears. "Well, I'm glad to see *some* young people have fashion sense nowadays."

Honey opened her mouth to make another excuse to get them the hell away from here—a desire everybody but Mrs. Lu shared, judging by Mr. Lu's sweaty demeanor, Buster's low growls, and Clarissa squeezing her iced coffee so hard it was seeping through the plastic lid.

Mrs. Lu stopped her with a hand on her arm. "While I have you here, I wanted to talk to you about your performance this weekend. I was *so* sad to hear you and

Ken broke up. But if you're better off as friends, then there's nothing you can do."

Honey nodded, imagining Sadie's eye-roll from inside the slide.

Mrs. Lu beamed, her perfect lipstick almost as red as her husband's healing cuts. "But I'm so glad you aren't letting a little breakup get in the way of your singing! You're so *talented*, Honey. And everything needs to be perfect for the party, and any last-minute changes would just—"

She mimed an explosion, breaking off into a laugh that got just a little too frantic.

Honey giggled with her, tugging her pigtails in a way she hoped was cute and not deeply stressed.

"*Honey*," Sadie whispered from the slide. "*I have a wad of gum in my hair. Make them leave!*"

"Well," Honey said, too loud. "I'll see you at the party! I can't wait to see your outfit. You too, Mr. Lu. Total bandage chic."

Buster barked, straining at the end of his leash. Trying desperately to get away.

"Buster!" Mrs. Lu tugged on the leash with an embarrassed laugh. "Looks like *somebody* wants to get back on his walk. See you, Honey. Nice to meet you...?"

She trailed off, looking at Clarissa expectantly.

"You too," Clarissa squeaked.

Mrs. Lu glanced at Honey, waiting for a name. Honey just kept smiling. Mrs. Lu smiled back, hesitant at first, then continued down the path.

No one spoke until the couple rounded the corner, Buster's whining fading the further he got from the playground.

A low curse drifted out of the slide. There was the sound of cracking plastic, and Sadie tumbled from its yellow mouth, landing feet-first in the bark.

"You *need* to cancel," she spat as she stood, fingers working at a wad of pink gum matted into her bangs. "Just because you want to be the life of the party—"

Honey groaned, rocking back and forth on the rusty swing. "It would be *suspicious*. Everyone who knows me knows I'd never let a little thing like a breakup and a weird viral video stop me from being fun and hot at a party. *Especially* if I'm getting paid."

Clarissa made a noise, laptop open in her arms, iced coffee poised on it once again. "Guys..."

"AND I'm pretty tight on money since I didn't work this summer and oh, yeah, I just got back from a road trip!"

"GUYS," Clarissa yelled. She was staring at her laptop screen, eyes wide. Her nervous sweat drowned out her cinnamon deodorant yet again.

"It's..." she said. "Um. He just messaged me?"

Sadie's sticky fingers paused in her hair. "Elijah?"

"Yeah."

They raced over. Clarissa squeaked as the girls blurred to a stop next to her, peering over her shoulder at the laptop screen. It was open to Elijah's Facebook page, a squinting photo with a plain white background that could double as his passport photo. His mustache was bigger, his beard longer, but it was definitely him.

A message from Elijah waited at the bottom of the screen:

*thinking you and me need 2 talk*

The laptop shook, iced coffee shaking on top of it. Clarissa was trembling.

"What do I say?" she squeaked. "Like—this is weird, right? He knows we're after him."

"He knows *you're* looking for him," Sadie said, teasing at the gum in her hair and wincing. "He knows you were threatening us in the woods. He knows I tried to kill you. You could say you—" She cut off with a frustrated groan. Gum tangled in her hair, sticking to her fingers. Every attempt to yank it out only mashed it deeper.

"God, Sadie, only idiots try to yank gum out of their hair," Honey told her, reaching to stop her futile efforts. "Are you an idiot? No! So quit it, we'll peanut butter it out later."

Sadie slapped Honey's hands away.

"I can't just ask him to leave us alone," Clarissa fretted, oblivious to what was rapidly becoming a slap fight in front of her. "What do I say?"

Honey ignored her, grabbing Sadie's wrist. It, too, was sticky. "God, how'd you get it on your *arm,* did you roll around in it?"

"Let *go!*" Sadie bared her teeth, shoving Honey back with enough force to send a human flying.

Honey stumbled into Clarissa, who shrieked as the iced coffee careened over. Coffee splashed onto the corner of her laptop keyboard, ice cubes rolling off to splatter onto everybody's shoes.

Honey whirled on her. "THIS is why you don't balance your drink on your laptop, dumbass!"

Clarissa whined, desperately holding her laptop upside down. More coffee splashed onto Sadie's shoes.

"Come on," Sadie snapped, jerking back.

"I'm sorry," Clarissa cried, righting her laptop and wiping at the wet keyboard. "No, half the keys don't work! I can't leave him on read, what do I do?"

"Shove it in a bag of rice," Honey suggested.

Sadie's eyes flashed black. "Say you want to help kill us!"

The park fell silent. Coffee dripped down Honey's legs.

"Um," Clarissa said. "What?"

# chapter
## nine

SADIE BRACED her homework against the steering wheel and stared.

"Multiply out of the brackets," Honey called from where she lay in the load space in the back of the van.

Sadie ignored her. She'd told Honey she was going to put effort into her schoolwork this year, but the homework was mostly so she could look like she was doing something if people looked in.

"Divide by zero," Honey continued. "Solve for x. Cross the $t$'s and dot the $i$'s."

"I can't hear you," Sadie said, gaze fixed on the paper on the steering wheel. "There's no one else in Steve-van but me. I'm doing my algebra homework and nobody's being annoying."

"Boo. Cross out Sadie."

Sadie didn't have to look in the rear-view mirror to know Honey was crossing the air. There was a low grunt as Honey shifted. The load space gave enough room to lie down, but not comfortably.

Honey asked, "How's the hair?"

"Oh shit, now you mention it," Sadie said flatly, "my hair combusted into flames. Oh, the pain."

Honey snickered. They'd bypassed the peanut butter solution and gone with cutting her bangs off. They'd regrown in an hour, but not before Honey took twenty photos and laughed herself stupid while Sadie tried to wrestle the phone from her.

The van fell into silence. For about ten seconds.

"Is he there yet?"

Sadie glanced up casually. They'd parked half a block down from a cafe. Clarissa had one of the outdoor seats, two empty glasses waiting in front of her. She fiddled with a suspender, hissing when it snapped back against her chest.

"Not yet," Sadie reported. "She keeps snapping her suspenders by accident."

Honey snorted. "It's like she never heard of breaking in a style before going outside in it. Like that one time you tried high heels and you had to walk around the mall with them in your hand."

Sadie groaned.

"What?"

"She's looking at us." Sadie glared at Clarissa, who was shooting them a nervous look from the cafe table. "Don't *look*, idiot."

She averted her eyes pointedly. When she glanced

back, Clarissa was fiddling with her new cellphone, staring at the empty glasses in front of her.

Honey started, "Does—"

"Shush! He's here."

Honey sat up in the load space, then immediately back down when Sadie gestured violently at her.

Sadie held her homework up, gaze trained just above the page. Half a block away, Elijah Harkner sat down in the tiny patio chair across from Clarissa.

"Does he have the toothpick?" Honey asked.

Sadie squinted. "He's in the exact same outfit. *Maybe* a different T-shirt. Same belt, same snakeskin boots, same dumb cowboy hat. I can't believe we got our asses kicked by a middle-aged dude in a cowboy hat."

"Can you hear what they're saying? Your vampire hearing is better."

Sadie sorely hoped not. Superhearing *sucked*. She focused on their mouths as they talked across the table, but the ambient noises drowned out their conversation —traffic, surrounding chatter, a dog barking in the next street.

"It's too far," Sadie said, and paused. "I could hear you yesterday. I heard it through all the noise in the cafeteria. You said my name."

Honey was quiet.

Sadie glanced in the rear-view mirror. There was no sign of Honey lying down behind the back seats, but Sadie could smell her: peach deodorant and apple conditioner. *I could eat you up*, Sadie told her on the last day of their trip, smoothing apple conditioner through her hair in a motel shower. Then she'd set her blunt teeth against Honey's wet shoulder.

Sometimes Sadie felt like that road trip was a wonderful, frightening dream. The moment they hit town limits she'd been gutted with loss. Like she'd wake up to see her own ceiling, a day of boredom and silence and day-drinking lying in dreaded wait.

"I was hoping," Honey said. "Like. You know penguins?"

"I've heard of them."

"They have this special song. If they're mates. They sing, and their mate will recognize it. Even if they're in a giant crowd of songs. They'll be able to pick it out."

It was the most romantic thing anyone had ever said to her. The paper blurred as black tears gathered at the corners of her eyes.

Sadie cleared her throat. "Not gonna lie, I was expecting an insect fact."

"Golden paper wasps can recognize each other by their faces."

"There we go," Sadie whispered.

She wiped her eyes. Her thumbs came back smudged with black eyeliner.

Honey asked, "What are they doing now?"

Sadie looked over the homework paper. Elijah leaned forward on his elbows, toying with his toothpick.

Clarissa was leaning back in her seat, thick arms wrapped protectively around her middle. She was smiling, but in that way girls smile when they want to be left the hell alone. Sadie felt a little bad for sending her into the belly of the beast. But they were in a public place. What was he going to do, pull that ankle knife on her right outside of a cafe?

He'd texted her new phone to suggest they meet in the woods.

*No thx,* Clarissa had sent back, Honey and Sadie looking over her shoulder. *No offense but idk if I can trust you since you shot me lol. Like I wanna help I don't want vamps in my town but you FULLY shot me.*

"Still talking," Sadie said.

"Boo. Let me know if he goes for the throat."

"Yeah? What do we do then? We can't go vampire on him in public."

"I don't know. Stab him with his own knife?" Honey shifted around, her shoe scraping against the van's blacked-out back window. "So, we can never start a band now."

"What?"

"If you were thinking about it," Honey continued. "If Honeybloods actually gave it a shot, we'd get hounded by true-crimers forever. Especially if they never catch the bassist, which, like. They're not *gonna.*"

Sadie curled the edge of her homework over. "I thought being a rock star was a stupid pipe dream for kids."

"Oh my god, you're actually *bitter*?" Honey's drawl made Sadie stiffen, paper crinkling in her fist. Then

Honey's voice softened. "Babe, everybody wants to be in a band when they're a kid. I also wanted to be an astronaut. I don't want those things *now*. I think…"

She trailed off. Sadie chewed her own tongue, fighting the urge to drip even more bitterness.

Honey blew out a breath. "I think I want to study bugs?"

Sadie blinked. She uncurled her hand from her homework. "Seriously?"

"Yeah." Honey let out a laugh, more bubbly than Sadie had heard in days. "What about you?"

Sadie stared down at her crumpled homework sheet. She hadn't even started the first question. Most of her teachers had done a double take when they watched her walk in on Monday. Not because they knew about the video, but because they hadn't expected to see her back for senior year.

"I don't know if college is for me," Sadie admitted.

Honey groaned, sitting up. "Sadie—"

Sadie cut her off. "He's leaving."

Honey dropped back to the van floor. Sadie stared intently at her homework, watching Elijah walk away out of the corner of her eye. She waited until he vanished from her peripheral vision, then looked up.

Clarissa was already rushing down the street toward them.

"Be *cool*," Sadie hissed uselessly.

Clarissa yanked the back door open and flung herself

into the back seats. "He is *so* freaky, oh my god. Wait, where's Honey? You said she was coming."

Honey sat up again. Clarissa shrieked.

"Shut *up*," said Honey and Sadie in unison.

Sadie threw her undone sheet of homework into the passenger's seat. "What happened? Did he buy that you wanted to help?"

"Yeah, I went on a whole thing about how, um, unnatural and dangerous you guys were." Clarissa rubbed her head. Honey had hit her hair claw, yanking her scalp. "I told him I can lure you into the woods on Saturday night. Same time and place as—"

"The last time he tried to kill us," Honey said flatly. "Awesome."

"So he shows up, I run away, you guys show up, and...?"

"Threaten him," Honey said instantly. "Cut off a limb or something. He'll leave."

Clarissa bit her nails, lost in thought. Sadie squirmed anxiously in the front seat. Did she buy it?

"I need another coffee," Clarissa announced, reaching for the van door. She climbed out onto the sidewalk, brushing sweaty strands of hair off her forehead. "Do you guys want...? Oh, sorry."

Then she slammed the van door shut. Another muffled *sorry* came through the metal for slamming it so hard.

Sadie twisted to look at Honey. "We're killing him, right?"

Honey barked a laugh, lying down on the backseat. "*Oh* yeah. Just need to get him away from Clarissa so he can't use her as leverage. You can go ham on someone again!"

She did a little series of claps, like she was suggesting a sleepover rather than a murder. But her eyes were too keen, almost worried.

"You hungry yet?" she asked.

*Always*, Sadie wanted to say. *I feel like any moment I'm not feeding is just...waiting for next time. Like nothing else matters. All my life's one big distraction from feeding.*

"Kinda," she replied.

Honey flipped her hair. "I'll go hunt later."

"I'll come," Sadie said. Then, when Honey tried to protest: "No, I'm coming. I can't...I need to learn how to control it."

Honey rolled her eyes and opened her mouth again.

Sadie cut her off. "What, you're gonna go fetch me raccoon blood every day forever? I *need* to control it."

Honey scoffed, like Sadie was overreacting. But Sadie could see the concern in her face, the way she couldn't quite meet Sadie's gaze.

chapter
## ten


"YOU JUST PULL YOURSELF OUT," Honey explained as they trekked further into the dark woods. "And then you trigger the venom. Like, blood is great. For a few seconds it's *everything*. But then it fades a little, and I get this tiny glimpse of me, Honey Williams, gorgeous vampire and Snow Fling Queen."

"That was in freshman year," Sadie told her. "*Little* sad that you're still rubbing it in everyone's face."

Honey thought about tripping her. It was less fun now they both had vampire reflexes.

Sadie stopped. "We're deep enough. If we go any further into these woods we'll start heading out the other side."

"Who died and made you woods expert?" Honey cocked her head, listening. No clumsy human shuffling through the dirt, no distant voices. They were on the edge of town. It was past eleven p.m. Nobody should be out here, especially not after the 'bear attack' that happened a few days ago.

"Do you think..." Sadie squeezed her eyes shut, shaking her head with a jerk. Trying to focus on something that wasn't hunger. "Do you really think you're gonna get prom queen this year?"

A month ago, Honey would've said *obviously*. There were girls who were more popular than her, even girls who were (arguably) hotter. But nobody had the untouchable quality of Honey Williams. Other girls were too fallible, too *human*: too-loud laughs or tripping in the hall or coming to class in the morning with their hair still wet. Not Honey. Her laugh was always on pitch, her gait steady and sexy, her hair ever-perfect. Most importantly, she didn't invite her classmates over or vent about arguments with her mom or cry on their shoulders during sad movies. She never let them in. When someone knew you, you stopped being larger than life and started being a person. You didn't want a person for prom queen—you wanted a symbol.

Other girls let people *know* them. Nobody knew Honey except Sadie Greer.

Honey flipped her ponytail. "Who else would they pick?"

"I don't know, someone who doesn't have murder rumors swirling—"

"The rumors will die. We'll start hanging out in a few months after everyone's forgotten about it."

"Hon—"

"You'll put up with Summer and Britney, and I'll be prom queen, and then we'll go to whatever school has scholarships in wildlife degrees."

Sadie was silent. Honey examined her nail polish. It was chipped. Chips in her nails grew back almost instantaneously, but chips in nail polish had to be fixed continuously.

Sadie said quietly, "I thought you were studying bugs."

"They don't offer that in freshman year," Honey replied. "You start off with wildlife, then you narrow it down."

She sucked in a breath. Bark, leaves, dry earth. There, beneath a bush: dusty fur.

Honey pointed. "There's a rat. Can I go first, or are you going to go all blood-frenzy and shove me out of the way?"

Sadie gave her a look with a level of sullenness usually reserved for put-upon twelve-year-olds. "Let's find out."

Honey winked. Then she darted forward, snagging the rat off the ground before it had time to take one tiny step. She drained it dry in two fast gulps, making sure not to let her disgust show as she let the limp rat drop to the ground, still warm.

"Yum," she said, barely strained. She readjusted her ponytail. "What next?"

Sadie pointed. "Two raccoons in a tree over there."

"One each." Honey beamed, licking rat blood off her teeth. "Race you."

Sadie took off. Honey ignored the desperation in her gait and chased her.

"Unfair," she called as they sprinted. "I didn't say—"

Sadie leapt, snatching the first racoon from the tree. Her teeth were in its throat before her bare feet hit the ground.

The second raccoon screeched, scrabbling up the tree trunk. Honey clambered up after it, glad for the blood-lust. It was easier to focus on than her meal's cute furry face.

She perched in a branch and drank.

"Sadie," she slurred against the raccoon's limp neck. "When we get changed back, are you going vegetarian?"

Sadie didn't answer, clutching her raccoon tight.

Honey hoped she didn't bring up the whole 'I can only get changed back if I murder you' thing. "Like," she continued. "It would make sense. But I think I won't. At least for chicken nuggets. That's *barely* meat."

Nothing.

Honey looked down. Sadie was still holding the raccoon, but she wasn't drinking. Her head was up, as still as a dog watching a rabbit as she stared into the woods. Alert. Listening.

Honey lowered the raccoon. Blood dripped down her chin.

"Sadie?"

Sadie twitched.

Honey focused. Insects gnawing on bark. Wind through leaves—

Sadie blurred into the trees.

"*Sadie!*" Honey jumped down and chased after her. The woods were pitch black, but it didn't matter— Honey could see the white of Sadie's tank top like a lodestar, shining through the trees.

*Please be a deer*, she thought as she dodged through the trees. *Please be a sad old deer with a paper cut.*

Honey strained. Wind rushed past her face. Branches grazed her skin and left no marks. Mosquitos buzzed, a squirrel chittered, somewhere far away an owl hooted.

Much less far away, somebody laughed.

Honey almost tripped over a rock. She knew that laugh.

She gritted her teeth and picked up speed. Sadie's white shirt glowed in the night, getting closer and closer to the voices. Soon Honey didn't have to strain to hear them.

"Clumsy bitch," said Britney, with a laugh she picked up from a reality TV show.

Summer squawked. "They shouldn't make the lid so sharp! Of course I'm gonna want to lick it as soon as I get tipsy!"

Sadie's hair flew out behind her in a dark wave. If Honey reached out, she could almost touch it.

"Well, now you have a bleeding tongue," Britney said. "Live with the consequences."

Too close. They were out of time.

Honey leapt. She caught Sadie around the waist, slamming her to the ground.

Sadie snarled and writhed. Honey shoved her harder into the dirt.

"*Don't make me cave your head in again*," she whispered.

Summer looked around. Honey could glimpse her silhouette through the trees. The two girls were sitting on a log, each of them holding a beer. A weak fire crackled between them.

"What was *that*?" Summer asked.

*Don't follow a strange noise into the woods, dumbass*, Honey thought as she wrestled Sadie facedown into the dirt. Sadie had all the strength of a feral vampire, but Honey was twice her size. It wasn't easy to pin her down, but she managed it.

Britney laughed. "Careful, it might be Honey waiting to rip your throat out!"

Beer bottles clinked. Sadie growled. Honey slapped a hand over her mouth and then abruptly pulled it away when Sadie tried to bite it.

"Don't joke about that," Summer said.

Britney snorted. "What, you believe your dad all of a sudden? Think Honey's gonna eat us both at the next sleepover?"

"Everybody knows it was a bear! *He* knows it's a bear. He felt so shitty when I told him that people are saying weird stuff about Honey."

Sadie writhed against Honey's tight hold. Honey dug her chin into Sadie's back, slapping a hand over her mouth again when Sadie whined.

Summer continued, "And like Honey would *ever* come to a sleepover. I just—it was funny for about five seconds, but there are people on the internet and even in town who are getting *creepy* about it. And you know how Honey gets when people say shit about her, I don't want to be around that. Remember when you said her new hair made her look like Willy Wonka?"

"No," said Britney curtly.

If this was any other situation, Honey would laugh. As it was, she kept holding Sadie down and hoped Sadie wouldn't become aware enough to get tactical about this. Honey didn't have actual fighting skills, just brute vampire strength and a deep desire to not see two of her frenemies die screaming.

"Come on," Summer coaxed. "She made you cry in front of everyone. She just—bam! *Right* for the throat."

"Yeah," Britney said admiringly. Then she coughed, a mocking tone returning to her voice. "Right for the throat is *right*. Munch munch."

"Dad got bit in the shoulder," Summer scolded. "By a *bear*."

Sadie twisted, struggling against Honey's grip. A snarl leaked out her throat, low and animalistic.

Summer stood. "Okay, I *definitely* heard something that time."

"Yeah, bitch, we're in the *woods*." Britney reached to poke the fire with a stick. "What you really want to be worried about is when it gets quiet. *That's* when you know things are gonna get—"

Sadie roared.

Britney and Summer shrieked, leaping up from the log and knocking over their drinks. Beer foamed over their shoes.

"Oh my god, bear bear *bear*," Summer yelped, backing away. "What do we—Britney! *Hey!*"

Britney was already running for it.

Summer cursed and ran after her. "You were just going to leave me to get *eaten*!"

"Hell yes, bitch," Britney screamed back.

The squirming under Honey was growing weaker. Sadie's growls quietened as Summer and Britney got further away.

Honey twisted Sadie's head to look her in the eye. "Are you normal again?"

Sadie winced. "Crap. Yeah. What did I do?"

"You scared the shit out of Summer and Brit." Honey stood up in one fluid motion and strode into the clearing where the fire was still flickering. She stomped it out fast.

Sadie lingered behind her, toeing at the beer bottles the girls had kicked over.

"Dumbasses," Honey said as she stomped the last embers into the dirt. "Who goes into the woods at *night*, to get *drunk*, two *days* after a bear attack?"

"Bored small-town kids." Sadie rubbed at her dirty cheek. Soil was smeared all down the side of her face. "Surprised they didn't tell you about it."

"They don't have to ask my *permission* to hang out,

Sadie. They're not toddlers. Besides, Brit knows I'm pissed at her."

Honey pinched a branch out of her hair. The downsides of not letting anyone close: everyone else broke off and got closer without you. They still hung out, of course. But Britney and Summer both knew Honey wasn't there for the real shit, the *deep* shit, life problems and worries and stresses. If they wanted to talk about that, they had each other. Honey was there to have fun and look hot.

Above them, a squirrel scurried up a branch, swift and quiet.

Not quiet enough. Sadie blurred up the tree, snatched the squirrel from its branch, and bit into its neck. She stayed like that, crouched in the tree like a gargoyle, until the squirrel was drained.

"There we go," Honey said when Sadie had finished sucking and growling. "Still hungry?"

Sadie climbed down the tree, dropping the squirrel corpse at their feet. She was still pale, shoulders slumped with exhaustion.

"Yeah," she said quietly. It sounded like *always*.

Honey watched her wipe blood off her chin. The girl she'd dragged into a bloody road trip, bitching the whole way. The girl who had stopped Honey in a bathroom to thank her for it. *You, like. Kind of saved me?*

Honey didn't feel like a savior.

IT WASN'T *ENOUGH*.

Sadie burst into the bathroom between classes. She listened for heartbeats, but the stalls were empty. All those heartbeats were out in the hall, a thrumming sea of heat and salt, waiting...

Sadie stalked into a stall and ripped her backpack open. She'd forgotten her pencil case today, but that didn't matter. What mattered was that she had a *thermos*. She uncapped it and inhaled, sucking in the not-quite-tantalizing scent of squirrel blood, before tipping it into her mouth.

Hot blood flowed down her throat. Sadie drank it greedily, licking warm smudges off the rim. Honey had tried explaining how thermoses regulated temperature last night while they were draining another unlucky animal into it, but Sadie hadn't been paying attention. She'd been too distracted by the last drips of the squirrel's blood slipping down the neck of the thermos.

She smacked it, trying to wring out the last drops. It still wasn't *enough*.

The bathroom door swung open. Sadie averted the last smack, standing deadly still in her stall as two girls spilled in, chatting loudly. Faucets turned on, water sloshing into the sinks.

"They heard something," said the first girl, whose name was Kitsey Bowers, a sophomore who broke her teammate's nose to get the winning volleyball shot last year. "Not a bear. Well, Summer said it was a bear, Britney said it totally wasn't."

The second girl sighed over the noise of pouring water. This was Daisy Verdan, a sophomore who looked up to the popular girls like they were her own personal reality TV show.

"Of course Summer would say that, she doesn't want anybody thinking her dad is crazy."

"*Is* he?" Kitsey asked. "Big difference between a bear and two girls."

"No way he's crazy! I've met him, he's super nice. It was definitely a bear. Even if he did see some girls, I think he just hallucinated. You can do that from stress sometimes."

Kitsey paused. "Or he's lying. He knows he'll seem crazy if he says it was girls, so he came up with a cover story."

Sadie curled her hands around the cooling thermos.

Daisy scoffed. "Whatever. I don't believe it's Honey. I

don't care if she hung out with Sadie Greer when they were kids, she'd never do it *now*."

"Right? *Ugh*. I heard she only washes her clothes once a month. What a freak."

Sadie's thermos creaked in her grip.

The water stopped. Kitsey continued, "Did you get an invite to Ken Lu's party tonight?"

"Nooo," Daisy said, footsteps heading for the door, "But I'm still gonna go. Like there's anything else to do in this town. Oh my god, did you hear they rented out Sapphire Palace? Supposed to be super fancy—"

The bathroom door swung shut.

Sadie held her thermos up to her mouth again. Still empty. There were dents in the metal, deep divots that fit her fingers perfectly.


The library was quiet when Sadie walked in, even though only a few students were using their free period to study. Everyone else was on their phones, one girl watching *Heartstopper* with her headphones in.

Honey sat on the other side of the room, Summer at her side. Ken and Britney sat opposite them, whispering and giggling in a way that made Sadie nervous. Honey ignored them, scrolling through her phone with a speed that meant she wasn't looking at anything.

Summer had a stack of college pamphlets splayed out in front of her and was flipping through them one by one.

Sadie's heart sank as she watched the stack grow. Since freshman year her future felt like a great dark pit she couldn't stop falling into. Then Honey came back into her life, and for a moment the future didn't seem so bad. But now it was looming in front of her again, deep and bottomless. She couldn't make out anything in the distance. Honey would go to college, and Sadie would... what?

She was so busy staring at the stack of pamphlets she didn't notice her classmates get up from Honey's table until it was too late.

"Okay," said Ken, tugging Sadie's headphones off as he slid into the seat next to her. "No audition. Just show up."

Britney beamed on the other side of her, jaw working around a wad of cherry gum. She'd never smiled at Sadie before in her life.

Sadie pulled her headphones back up. They didn't even have time to settle before Ken was tugging them away again.

"Please?" He pouted. "All the cool kids have live music at their parties. *Fully* live, not just a singer with music playing over the speakers. I'll be the laughingstock of the *school* if I don't get you. Right, sis?"

Summer flipped him off without looking up from her stack of pamphlets.

"Brutal." Ken turned back to Sadie, still pouting. "Help me, Sadie-Wan Kenobi, you're my only hope!"

Sadie glared at him.

Britney leaned in, breathing her cherry gum stink all over Sadie's face. It was almost preferable to her usual stink, which made Sadie want to lean in and bite her.

"Sadie," she said conspiratorially, like she and Sadie were old friends sharing a secret. Like Sadie didn't already have one of those, impossibly bigger than any weak secret Britney could cough up.

"I don't have to tell you how boring this town is," Britney whispered. "When something finally happens, we gotta make the most of it. Last month it was Geraldine Simmons getting pregnant with her best friend's brother and running away to Ohio. Right now, it's you. Is it a weird internet rumor? Do monsters walk among us? Honestly, I don't care. I just want *something* to *talk* about. Hey, if you had nothing to do with those murders or Mr. Lu getting attacked, then you've got nothing to worry about. *And* you get a hundred bucks. Right, Ken?"

Ken stroked a thumb down Britney's wrist. "You should be a lawyer, babe. That was so hot."

Britney giggled, twisting her hand so their fingers brushed.

Sadie watched their skin touch, warmth against warmth. *You just ate,* she told herself as their pulses beat louder in her ears. *You're not hungry. You're* not.

Honey twisted in her seat. "You know she's only flirting with you because I had you first, right? She's dated, like, four of my exes. She thinks you're a conceited loser. Dating me first is your *only* appeal."

Summer shushed her and glanced toward the corner where Mr. Halbert sat behind a desk, playing Tetris with earbuds in. He didn't look up from his phone.

Britney's eyes lit up. "You sound jealous. Why, want him back?"

"I'd rather have a Tabasco enema. You know, it's funny that you want to be interesting so bad, but you can't seem to find any way to do it that doesn't involve me." Honey beamed. "Anyway, you're free to have my leftovers."

Britney glared at her. She recovered quickly, reaching up to flick Sadie's boxy black bangs. "Does Sadie count as leftovers?"

Sadie didn't dare breathe. Britney's wrist was so *close*, the pulse fluttering underneath her thin skin. Excited by the sport. Sadie wanted to tell Britney they were on totally different playing fields. Wanted to warn her of her sharp teeth. Mostly, though, she wanted to slam her down on the desk and sink her teeth in.

Honey scoffed, pulling Sadie back into reality.

"I have not talked to Sadie Greer in a million years," Honey hissed. "Do whatever you want with her."

With that, she turned back to her phone.

Sadie swallowed.

On one side of her, Ken sniggered. "Wow. Hear that, Brit? We can do whatever we want."

Sadie curled her hands into fists, consumed by how easy it would be to break his jaw. Screw school, screw secrecy, screw Honey telling her assholes to *do whatever they want,* Sadie was so *hungry.*

Britney took Sadie's bangs and pulled, almost soft, running her fingers down the strands. Still with that smug smile, like she had the upper hand here. Like she wasn't a mouse in front of a snake.

Sadie moved. Too fast, too *strong,* shoving Britney back with such force it lifted Britney's chair underneath her. Britney went sprawling, rolling three times before coming to a dazed stop on the library carpet. The chair slammed a table, making the occupants jump.

For a moment, nobody spoke. Honey stared, mouth open, nothing but shock written across her tanned face. Like she really didn't give a shit what anyone did to Sadie.

Then the room burst into noise, Britney crying something about her wrist and Ken rushing to help her, throwing a dismissive, "Bitch!" back at her as he crouched down to help. Summer followed him, scattering her college pamphlets to the ground in her haste. Mr. Halbert got up, earbuds still in, asking what the hell just happened.

Sadie listened, unmoving, to their heartbeats, a great rising storm pounding her eardrums, louder and louder. She didn't look at Honey again, unsure what she'd do if she saw Honey giving her the same look everybody else was aiming at her, all that disgust and shock and, for some, genuine fear. For every doubter, there had to be a few who believed Sadie really did have something to do with the murders and Mr. Lu's attack. By the looks of it, Sadie was on her way to convincing a few more.

Sadie had only been in the principal's office once before, two years ago, when her grades got so bad her dad was called in to discuss what should be done. It looked the same: boring white walls, motivational posters with kittens, a pine-scented air freshener spritzing on an automatic timer from the top shelf of an Ikea bookcase.

Principal Acorn waved her into the office impatiently. He was wearing the same ill-fitting suit he always wore, with a different tie depending on the day. Today it was cheesecake yellow.

"Obviously you're suspended," he told her as she sat in the stiff wooden seat in front of his desk. "I have to say, this is the first time somebody's managed to get themselves suspended in the first week."

Sadie didn't reply. She was trying to remember if she had any alcohol stashed around the house, or, failing that, if she could be bothered shoplifting from Cooper's Corner on the way home.

Principal Acorn adjusted his toupee. It was decent. Sadie wouldn't be able to tell if he didn't adjust it so much.

"Should I be expecting anything else like this, Miss Greer?"

Sadie shook her head.

He sighed. "I don't know what happened to you,

Miss Greer, I really don't. Your middle school teachers said you were a model student. I had you pegged for the honor roll. Now the one good thing about you is that you don't cause trouble. Sure, you were useless in class, but you kept your head down. Didn't make waves. Now look at you—spraining Britney's wrist! I'm going to be stuck in this office for hours listening to her mother yell at me for letting this happen, I hope you know that."

Sadie picked at her sleeves. More stupid flannel. She'd picked it because it was comfortable, and over time she'd grown attached. Now she wasn't sure if it was a good attachment or the attachment that had her going over her booze stashes in her head. Sadie was so sick of ruining herself, but in her defense, she'd gotten pretty good at it.

Principal Acorn shook his head. "To be honest, I don't even know why you came back for senior year."

Sadie shrugged. She wanted to cry, but she'd rather break her own wrist than do it in the principal's office. Also, she couldn't start crying big black tears in front of him without him calling in a hazmat squad.

"Maybe I want to be better," she mumbled.

"Well," Principal Acorn said curtly, "You're off to a bad start."

## twelve

HONEY SLAMMED the front door open.

"Hope you're hungry for squirrel blood, bitch, 'cause…" she trailed off. "Hi."

Clarissa waved. She was on the couch, TV switched to *Gilmore Girls*, wearing the first pair of leg warmers Honey had seen in real life.

"Thank god you're here!" Clarissa placed her laptop carefully on the couch and bounced up. "Sadie's feeling a bit, um. She's throwing up. I think she's drunk. *Very* cool you guys can still eat and drink, I'd go crazy if I couldn't have coffee!"

"We can't," Honey said. She took a thermos out of her handbag and twirled it. It was shiny with Honey's spit. It had been thoroughly licked clean after squeezing the squirrel blood into it. Draining an animal into a small hole was not as easy as Honey would have assumed a month ago.

"I got blood on the way over," Honey said as Clarissa

tried to ask the next logical question. "Unless you want to contribute."

Clarissa laughed nervously.

A loud retching noise echoed down the hall.

"God, I was *joking*," Honey assured Clarissa. She pinched Clarissa's chubby cheek, then set off toward the Greer bathroom.

The door was locked. Honey rattled the doorknob hopefully.

"Go away," Sadie groaned.

Honey didn't let go of the doorknob. "You know I can break this, right? Don't make me break another one of your doors, babe. You know I'll do it."

"Don't call me—" Sadie cut off, gurgling.

Honey grimaced. Her hand tightened. "Five seconds or I break the door."

"You are such—" More gagging. The sound of Sadie crawling clumsily across the bathroom tiles.

The door swung open.

Honey cocked her hip. "There. Was that so hard?"

Sadie flipped her off. She was already crawling back to the toilet, dropping her face back into the bowl.

Honey twirled the thermos. "Look what I brought. Tasty, tasty squirrel blood."

"Leave me alone," Sadie mumbled.

"Tried that," Honey reminded her. "Didn't go great."

She sat down next to the toilet. The floor was just as

dusty as last time, and Honey couldn't remember where she'd left her lint roller.

"Went…" Sadie burped. "Went great for you. You're *popular*. You're *fun*. You're *stupidly* hot."

Honey preened, setting the thermos and her handbag down by Sadie's knees. "Thankies."

"No, I'm insulting you. This is an insult." Sadie stiffened, clutching her stomach. "*Ugh*."

Honey rubbed her back awkwardly. Before Sadie, she'd never patted someone's back while they threw up. Britney and Summer had given her the opportunity a few times, but she'd never taken them up on it.

"There there," she said as Sadie retched into the toilet. "Get it aaaaall out, babe."

"Don't call me babe!" Sadie twisted to swat at Honey's hand on her back. "Quit it."

Honey dropped her hand. "Are we going to do this every time you get upset," she asked sourly. "Like, you get a bad mark on a test and I'll come over and find you puking your guts out? What'd you do this time, try beer instead? It's all gonna end up the same way."

Sadie rested her cheek on the toilet seat. "Are you going to Ken's party?"

"I don't have to."

Sadie glowered. "You *want* to go. You wanna be hot and sing and have a fun, hot time."

"I want to not be suspicious," Honey added. She brushed Sadie's bangs away from her face, only doubling down when Sadie pulled away. "I won't go if you need me."

Sadie looked up at her: a wet, stinging glare. The last time she'd looked at Honey like that, Honey had her pinkie raised in an attempt at forgiveness. Sadie had slapped it away and run out of the room, and they hadn't talked until Honey burst into her living room asking Sadie to help her bury a body.

Honey's stomach twisted in panic.

"I won't," she repeated. *You can't go, either. Don't run away again.*

Sadie lurched up, grabbing the thermos. "Go," she said, unscrewing the lid.

Honey hesitated.

"Go," Sadie repeated. She took a swig and shivered in disgust. "Go on, *go.*"

Honey thought about rolling her eyes. About finding a non-vulnerable way to say, *you'll be here when I get back, right? I won't come back and find the doors locked?*

"Remember to rate me five stars on Uber Eats," she said finally.

Sadie frowned up at her. "What?"

"Blood delivered right to your bathroom door," Honey said nonsensically, and closed the door behind her.


The retching sounds slowly died down.

This was good. It meant Honey didn't need to go for another blood run after she put her makeup on.

Clarissa appeared in Sadie's bedroom doorway as Honey applied her second coat of eyeshadow.

"Heeeey," Clarissa said, fiddling with her leg warmers. "You're going out? That's cool. I'll just be here. Ordered a pizza. Gonna watch *Gilmore Girls*. I got Sadie monologuing about it and now I'm kinda hyped. What season should I start with?"

It was such a ridiculous question Honey had to put her brush down and stare at her. "What? One."

Clarissa snorted. "Yeah, but when does it get good?"

Honey stared some more.

"Okay, TV purist." Clarissa's phone vibrated in her leg warmer. She dug it out, and her eyes widened. "Oh shit, Elijah texted me."

Honey reached for her makeup bag, searching for her lip gloss. "Giving up?"

"He asked if we're still on for luring you into the woods tomorrow." Clarissa's thumbs blurred across the phone screen. "I'm saying yes. Obviously. He also asked where I'm staying. As if I'd *tell* him that."

Her phone continued to buzz, one notification spilling in after the other.

"Popular girl," Honey commented.

Clarissa shook her head. "Oh, this is just... commenters."

She paused, strangely abashed. For a second Honey had thought Clarissa would lie, and say they were friends asking how she was doing after taking off suddenly. She didn't seem like someone who could pull that off.

Clarissa bit her lip. Of the several versions Honey had witnessed—spookytimegirlies04 Clarissa and Detective Chic Clarissa—this one looked the most real. PJ shorts and bulky leg warmers. Frizzy dark hair damaged from continuous straightening and a T-shirt so baggy it could belong to Sadie.

"I wanted to say," Clarissa blurted. "I...I think you guys are really great together. It's such a good *story*, you know? Childhood friends reunited, falling in love. Killing and dying for each other."

"You can't do a video on us," Honey said.

"I wouldn't," Clarissa said, too fast. She'd obviously been thinking about it. "I only meant...it makes my dating life seem really pathetic. Not that I've dated much. I don't know if my friends-with-benefits situation with my chem partner or that girl I went on three Tinder dates with counts."

Honey didn't know what to say to that.

"Hot," she said finally.

"It makes my friendships seem kind of stupid too," Clarissa continued. "I don't have friends who would drop everything to go on a murder road trip with me. I don't have friends, period. I think that's why I like online communities so much? Everybody's talking to me. Everyone wants to know what I think."

She shrugged, a small, timid smile on her lips. So earnest and embarrassed under all her flimsy YouTuber charisma. If she'd gone to Honey's high school, Honey would've made fun of her on sight.

The back doorbell rang.

Clarissa let out a sigh of relief. "Thank *god*, I was so hungry. Oooh, that was *way* earlier than the app said it'd be. Five stars."

She flounced off toward the back door, still embarrassed and not doing a great job at hiding it.

Honey wondered if that was how she looked in those rare moments she let people glimpse her heart, and grimaced. She turned back to the mirror and smoothed on lipstick. Bright red. She read the name on the tube.

*HONEYBITES*, it declared in thick black letters. A sixteenth birthday gift from Britney, given to her in the woods. Fairy lights strung up every tree, Honey blasting pop music from Bluetooth speakers, surrounded by people who wanted her approval and didn't give a shit about her.

*It reminded me of you,* Britney told her slyly when she handed the lipstick over.

Honey had grinned up at her with all her blunt, human teeth and felt so bored and empty she had to fight back a scream. She only had hazy memories after that— kissing a college guy, kissing a girl she didn't remember anything about except her strawberry lip gloss. Trying to wrestle with Summer and getting rebuffed, shutting Summer down when she tried to tell Honey how worried she was about an upcoming exam; dancing and puking and skinning her knees. Mostly she remembered turning the music up louder and louder until she could no longer hear her own voice singing along.

Honey smacked her lips and smiled. Her reflection smiled back at her, bright and sexy and not at all trembling.

"Still got it," she told herself.

Clarissa screamed.

Honey bolted out, makeup cascading from her handbag as she sprinted for the back door.

A familiar voice stopped her in her tracks.

"You think I'm stupid," snarled Elijah over Clarissa's begging. "I know they're here! You're on their side!"

"Shit," Honey whispered.

The bathroom door flew open behind her. Sadie lurched out, black ooze smeared down her chin.

Honey stabbed a finger at her. "Get back in there."

"What? But—"

"You look like you'll fall over if he breathes on you," Honey hissed. "Don't come out unless I say!"

Sadie scowled. "It's my house!"

"Stay," Honey told her, and ran for the back door.


Elijah had a knife at Clarissa's throat and a crossbow at his side. He whipped it in Honey's direction as soon as Honey stepped out, the weapon gleaming in the moonlight.

"Please," Clarissa gasped, straining against his grip. "It's all cool, they're fine, everything's fine—"

She cut off with a whimper as Elijah pressed the knife roughly against her skin. His cowboy hat was askew, beady eyes drilling into Honey as he leveled the crossbow at her heart.

Honey raised her hands. "Elijah. Hi. Nice to meet you officially. I'm Honey—"

"Where's the other one?"

"I don't know," Honey blurted.

"This is her *house*. I've been *watching*. Where is she?"

"I don't know," Honey lied. She swallowed. "I really like your cowboy hat. Where'd you get it?"

He scowled at her. "You think I'm playing? She comes out or the kid dies."

He pressed the knife harder. Blood beaded at its silver tip, and Honey's mouth watered.

"She's human," Honey tried, listening desperately for any sounds of Sadie about to go feral inside the house. "Don't you have a code or something? *Thou shalt not harm innocent civilians caught in a vampire's stupid shit?*"

"Or she dies," Elijah repeated.

Honey concentrated. His heartbeat was up, his armpits damp with panic. Still no sign of Sadie about to barrel outside with her fangs bared.

*Stay*, Honey thought.

"They didn't hurt anyone," Clarissa tried, standing on her tiptoes to lessen the knife's pressure. "Except that band, but they were vampires too, they practically did your job for you! And that guy in the woods, they didn't kill him when they totally could've! They won't hurt anyone else, I promise!"

"They always do," Elijah said darkly. His finger crept toward the crossbow trigger. "Where is she?"

Honey's mind raced. There was no way out of this with all of them intact.

Elijah's finger curled around the trigger, not yet squeezing. "Where *is* she?"

A drop of blood rolled down the knife. Clarissa whimpered.

Honey opened her mouth.

A car turned down the street. Honey tensed. She knew that choppy rumble.

"What?" Elijah barked. "What's—"

Munson's car turned down the driveway. Honey gave it thirty seconds before Munson came in through the front.

Elijah swore. His grip tightened on the knife.

"She comes with me," he said. "One hour. Find your girl, you two show up where I say, and she goes free. You don't show—she dies."

"Hot," Honey croaked. "I mean, okay. Yes. We'll be there."

Elijah dragged Clarissa out the back gate. Clarissa tripped over her own feet, and Honey heard a small squeak of *sorry!* before they disappeared down the street.

Honey dug her fingers into her palms, tight enough to break human skin. Shit. *Shit.*

Sadie blurred outside, glaring at the open back gate. "We're letting him get away?"

Honey gestured at her angrily. "You're falling over where you stand! He kicked our ass last time, what was I supposed to do?"

The front door slammed. Heavy footsteps. Munson Greer's voice echoed through the house: "Oh. Hey. I'm making dinner, you girls sticking around?"

The girls stared at each other. Honey's lips flinched. Sadie's lips tightened. A full conversation in the smallest of facial features.

"No," Sadie yelled back. "We have somewhere to be."

# chapter
## thirteen

THE PHONES LAY side by side on Sadie's bed, still and dark and stubbornly silent. Clarissa's pizza box sat untouched on the pillow. It had been half an hour since Elijah dragged Clarissa off the back porch. They were still waiting for him to let them know where to go.

Sadie swore and grabbed her phone.

"She's hours away," Honey said for the third time tonight, curled up against the mirror. "Even if she picks up, what's she gonna do?"

"Better than just sitting here," Sadie snapped, scrolling into Recent Calls. She clicked Milly's name. It rang.

*Click.* "Hi, this is Milly Hart. I can't come to the phone right now—"

Sadie threw the phone down and shoved an arm under her mattress.

Honey sat up. "What are you doing?"

"Nothing. Shut up." Sadie produced a half-empty bottle of whiskey. Not her usual pick, but in the store Cooper kept side-eyeing her from the counter, and it was the closest thing she could sneak into her backpack.

Honey snatched it from her. "Oh, great! You wanna be even more useless when we gotta go save Clarissa? Gonna be all, *unhand her, jackass...*" She mimed puking all over the floor, only stopping when Sadie dove for the bottle in her hand.

"Quit it," Sadie snapped, grabbing for it. Sadie had height, but Honey had strength, holding Sadie away easily.

Sadie growled, still straining. "You're such a *baby*!"

"I don't have time to go out hunting again, so unless you want to bite dear old dad—"

They paused as Fleetwood Mac's 'Landslide' pounded through the wall.

Honey snorted. "Woooow. I forgot he used to hole up in his room and listen to Dad music when we were being loud."

Sadie lunged. Honey jerked back just in time, too fast. The glass bottle smacked Sadie's bedpost and shattered, whiskey spilling onto the pillow, dripping down the wood, and soaking the carpet.

Honey stared down at the shattered bottle neck she was holding, stepping away so the growing stain didn't reach her shoes.

"Great," she sighed, dropping the broken bottle on Sadie's bed. "*Now* look what you did."

Sadie wanted to cry. She wanted to scream. She wanted her room to be still and silent again, where nothing could hurt her but herself. Tears built up behind her eyes, cold and mortifying.

"I was so scared to come back here," Sadie said, voice cracking. "You said everything would be fine. Guess what? NOT FINE, HONEY! This SUCKS! Being a vampire SUCKS!"

Honey laughed, high and nervous, reaching to squeeze Sadie's cheeks. "Aw, big baby needs—"

Sadie shoved her. Honey fell back onto the bed, narrowly missing the broken bottle and both their phones.

"Could you take something seriously for FIVE SECONDS," Sadie screamed. "Why is it so hard for me and not for you? We were supposed to hang out at school, things were supposed to be different! I hate it here! I can hear everything people say about me, and suddenly *everybody's* saying shit!"

The Fleetwood Mac music got louder.

"SHUT UP," Sadie screamed at the wall. Below her, Honey squirmed. But still with that faint, unsure smile, like she could find some way to make Sadie laugh and forget about all of this. Like all the world's problems could be solved by Honey rolling her eyes and flashing a condescending smirk.

Sadie bared her teeth. "You know what? Maybe you DID ruin my life."

Honey flinched. She looked shocked, but only for a

moment. Then something else flooded in: resignation. Like she'd been expecting this. But still trying to smother it, still trying to look hot and cool and casual, mouth twisting as she tried to keep smiling.

Neither of them spoke. Fleetwood Mac boomed through the wall. They were on the verse about children getting older, which always made Sadie emotional for reasons she didn't understand, and today was no exception.

Sadie wiped a black tear off her cheek. "Hon—"

Honey's phone rang.

They stared at it. The screen was lit up next to Honey's elbow: *CLARISSA*.

Honey grabbed it. "Hello?"

"There's an abandoned house at 22 Pearl Street. Know it?"

"Yes," Honey said. Sadie couldn't tell if she was lying.

"Meet me there in twenty minutes. If the both of you don't come, she dies. Got it?"

"Totally," Honey said. "One hundred percent. Crystal clear. We..."

She trailed off, clenching her jaw.

*What?* Sadie mouthed. She tried to get Honey's attention, draw her gaze away from Sadie's soaked pillow. Honey didn't look at her, clenching the phone so hard Sadie feared it would shatter.

Then all at once, her hand loosened. Honey's smile came back, bright and bitchy.

"Actually, you know what? No thankies."

Silence. Sadie stared at Honey desperately, mouthing *what the hell are you doing*? Honey ignored her and twirled a strand of hair around her pinkie.

"I will *kill* her," Elijah said, incredulous.

"Yeah. Boo." Honey examined her nails. "Sucks for her. Anyway, me and Sadie are gonna go eat some folk. 322 Drow Lane, in the field behind that big parking lot. Byeeee."

Sadie stared as Honey ended the call, frowning at the phone.

"You know," Honey said, "Sometimes I wish we lived through the era of flip phones. They looked so *satisfying* to hang up with. Like, *fuck you*, click click bitch."

"Pretty sure there was just one click," Sadie said weakly. She crouched in front of Honey, finally drawing her gaze. "Honey. What the HELL did you just do?"

Honey shrugged, still twisting hair around her pinkie. "We're never gonna beat him on his own playing field, Sadie. He'll set up traps and shit. If we're fast, *we* can set up traps."

"At your ex's birthday party? In a *barn*?"

"Excuse you, it's a very fancy event space—"

"It's a renovated barn, they're still pulling hay out of the floorboards."

Honey stood up, heading for her handbag. Sadie caught her wrist.

"Honey," she said. "*What* are we doing?"

Honey stared down at her. For a moment her eyes shuttered, a reminder of the fight they'd been dragged out of thanks to the phone call. Then she smiled, not bright but at least a spark.

"Get your guitar."

chapter
## **fourteen**

SAPPHIRE PALACE OPENED six months ago. It hosted weddings, bar mitzvahs, and lavish Christmas celebrations that employers put on instead of giving their workers a raise. And as of tonight, rich kids' birthday parties.

The main room had two small windows and made up for this with a hundred lights dangling from the ceiling. White flowers hung between them, their plastic petals warped by the heat from the lights. And in the middle of everything: a giant glossy *18*, too heavy to spin in the AC breeze.

Honey stared up at it, considering. It *looked* heavy enough to kill someone. Ropes connected it to the ceiling, running through a pulley and ending in a thick knot on the wall. If somebody undid that knot...

"You made it!"

Honey turned. Ken Lu nodded at her with a stupid smug look, hair bigger than ever.

"Party's about to get started," he told her. "Was getting worried you wouldn't show. Should've known you'd never miss a good party."

"Yeah, well. We'll see if this is a good party." Honey pointed at the stage jutting out of the opposite wall. A microphone stand was already set up, a neat box sitting next to it. "Everything ready for me?"

"You know it." He bounced on his heels, expensive sneakers squeaking on the polished floorboards. "Sooo... it's the tracklist we talked about. Plus the happy birthday song at the start. You remember—"

"I remember." Honey glanced through the thin crowd, people still piling in, milling near the drinks table. The punch had already been spiked, Honey could smell it from here. Whiskey, the same brand that she'd spilled all over Sadie's floor.

"Great. We have your outfit..." Ken trailed off, staring at something over Honey's shoulder.

Honey didn't have to look. She knew who it was.

She turned anyway, forcing her face into vague, uncaring surprise.

"Huh," she said.

Sadie looked even more pale and weak than she did at school. She was wearing the same jeans and flannel shirt, though her eyeliner was gone. She looked younger without it, and oddly vulnerable.

"Sadie," Ken said. "You're...here?"

"You said it was a hundred bucks." Sadie hitched her guitar strap up her chest. "Right?"

Mrs. Lu appeared through the sparse crowd, a rictus smile fixed on her face.

"Sweetheart, hi, so glad you're here," she said to Honey, voice too high. Her gaze darted to Sadie and her guitar. "Ken, didn't I say no last-minute changes? We have your Spotify playlist ready to—"

"It's my birthday, mom," Ken said, running a hand through his tall hair. He kept blinking at Sadie, bewildered. He'd never actually expected her to show up.

Mrs. Lu clenched her teeth, still smiling. "Right. Yes. It *is* your big day."

"It's fine," Ken told her, barely holding back his annoyance. "Go see if the glasses are clean yet."

Mrs. Lu gave them all a tight nod and rushed off.

Ken looked at Sadie, some of that smug look returning. "Honey can tell you the set list. If she's cool with this."

Honey shrugged. "Free country."

Ken looked disappointed. "Cool. Whatever. Uh, there's no amp, but go set up, I'll get your money ready for after."

Sadie was already walking toward the stage. Honey followed, watching the guitar strung behind Sadie's back. Those familiar brown tones, their initials cut into the wood so many years ago: *SG + HW 4EVA*. They'd carved it with an earring. Honey couldn't remember whose.

Sadie climbed up onto the stage, slinging the guitar around until she could hold it.

"You haven't told me the rest of the plan," she whispered as she strummed a few chords.

Honey looked over at the knot which held the giant *18* looming over all their heads. It was in plain sight, lodged on the wall next to the hallway.

"I'm still thinking."

"Well, hurry up. A true crimer's life depends on it." Sadie's fingers stilled on her chords. "What am I playing?"

Honey got out her phone and showed her the Spotify playlist.

Sadie leaned down to examine it. "Lotta drums in these. Probably be better if they play the instrumentals."

"But then you won't be here and they won't have anything to whisper about," Honey told her, fitting her phone back into her pocket. "Pass me that box next to the mic. I need to change."

Sadie handed it down. Their hands did not brush.

"Thanks," Honey said, calm and unaffected. More people were filing in now, everybody's gaze drawn to the only interesting gossip that had happened to this town in years. Before the road trip, they'd ignored each other for years. It felt almost natural to avoid each other's gazes as Honey turned away.

"If he arrives while I'm in there," Honey whispered, lips barely moving as she walked away, "say *Honeybloods.* I'll hear it."

"Got it," Sadie whispered back.

More people were filing in. Honey gave them a quick

glance, unnoticed as everybody stared and whispered at Sadie tuning her guitar onstage. There was only one door into Sapphire Palace, and it was also the only way out. For all their lavish furnishings, they'd forgotten to put in an emergency exit.

Summer and Britney squeezed through the door, coming to a dead halt when they spotted what everyone was staring at. Summer's mouth fell open. Britney's hand flew to her injured arm, which was covered with a brace. It was black and ugly and didn't match her sleek red dress at all.

The two girls noticed Honey next, and immediately made a beeline for her. Their classmates, who had been stuck behind them as they gaped, resumed their forward march.

Honey shifted the box under one arm so she could wave. "The prodigal copycat returns. Surprised you could make it."

"Of course I'm here. It's Ken's *birthday*." Britney gave her a stiff smile, like she actually gave a shit about Ken before Honey started dating him. Her jaw worked anxiously around a wad of cherry gum.

"He *is* my brother," Summer said, much more obvious with her unenthusiasm. "I kind of have to be here. Even though your arm is *definitely* a good enough excuse for us to ditch this, go to your place and watch *Drag Race*—ow! Don't step on me, I *will* twist your arm!"

Honey snickered, wishing she could enjoy this more.

She so rarely got to see a good old-fashioned Summer–Britney bickering match. They'd been friends years before Honey came along, and had gotten most of their fights out of the way before high school.

Britney pointed at the stage with her good hand. "I can't believe she showed up. You're actually going to sing with her?"

"Bit late to back out now." Honey hoisted her box back in front of her. "I need to get changed. Try not to break your other wrist while I'm gone."

"It's sprained," Britney called after her. "By your freaky *friend*!"

Honey ignored her. She was still focused on the stage she didn't dare look at, waiting for Sadie to whisper *Honeybloods*.

The dress was fine. Not Honey's usual style, but she could make anything look good. She did a few spins, watching the white skirt flare out and smack into the toilet stalls. This bathroom was not made with dress flares in mind.

She headed through the narrow hallway that led back to the main room. It was empty except for one girl with a familiar black bob.

"People are taking photos of me," Sadie said, clutching her guitar like a kid with a teddy bear. She frowned. "What are you *wearing*?"

Honey readjusted her boobs. "It's not just happy

birthday, it's *happy birthday Mr. President.* Except I'm singing *Mr. Ken-i-dent.*"

Sadie looked pained. "Man. Hope Elijah kills us before then."

She glanced behind her. The hallway had a single window facing the field that doubled as a parking lot. Sadie watched another car pull in, and Honey knew she was thinking about Steve-van parked a block over, waiting.

Bitterness rose in Honey like a wave. "You're not going to run again, right? After this, you're not gonna storm out and start ignoring me?"

Sadie grimaced. "I—"

"Because that'd be really shitty of you," Honey said over her. "I know I'm...I *know*, okay? But I'm trying. Opening up, or whatever. If that's what it takes to keep you."

Sadie hunched over her guitar. "You want me to stay?"

"I always want you to stay, dumbass," Honey hissed. "I wanted you to stay then, I want you to stay now, I don't CARE if we fight, I want..."

She stopped, swallowing the horrible lump in her throat, and with it the instinct to double back and turn this into a joke. You could deal with anything if it was a joke, especially if you made the other person feel small.

"I want *you*," she admitted quietly. "My best friend. My fucking *girlfriend*. But if you really think I ruined your life—"

"I don't." Sadie said. "I shouldn't have…"

Her hand tightened on her guitar, thumb brushing the initials they'd carved so many years ago. "I meant it, back in that bar bathroom. Going on that road trip saved me. I had years of…of this deep, awful boredom and drinking alone in my room like a loser and not talking to *anyone*. Seriously, it was so bad, Hon. Then you came bursting back in, and yeah, okay, some of it has sucked but not you. You're good. A good thing in a…in a shitty situation."

Honey felt herself nod mutely, watching the window behind Sadie's head. Honey couldn't look at her directly or she'd have to go back and fix her makeup. A truck pulled into view. Old and red and covered in dried mud. Blacked-out windows. It slid aggressively into a spot that, until a moment ago, was about to be filled by a Toyota.

The Toyota beeped. A man's hand flashed out the truck's window, the engine rattling to a stop.

Sadie asked, "What? What is it?"

Honey dragged Sadie away from the window, tucking them out of sight along the hallway.

"He's here," she told Sadie, mind racing. "I'm gonna go distract him."

"Hon—"

"What's he going to do in a room full of witnesses? You go out there, see if he has Clarissa."

Sadie nodded, pulling back. Honey caught her shoulder.

"You know that giant *18* hanging in the middle of the ceiling?"

Sadie nodded again.

"Great," Honey said, taking both of Sadie's shoulders now, looking into those big green eyes and only wanting to cry a little. "Know how there are no emergency exits?"

# fifteen

SADIE CREPT around the side of Elijah's truck and peered in.

No dice. Vampire sight didn't help with blacked-out windows. But she still had super hearing, and her vampire ears could clearly hear a muffled whimper coming from the backseat.

She knocked on the window, soft and fast.

The whimpering stopped.

Sadie winced. "Clarissa?"

A loud squeaky grunt.

"Taking that as a yes," Sadie whispered. "Don't worry, we're gonna get you out of there."

She peeked around the truck, waiting for the last few teens to trickle out of the parking lot and into Sapphire Palace. Then she punched the back window out.

Glass rained onto the backseat. Clarissa yelped, muffled by the gag in her mouth. She pulled her legs up with the leg warmers clumped down by her ankles. Her hands were bound behind her back. Mascara streaked her cheeks and her shiny black hair was frizzy from rubbing over the leather seat.

"Hi," Sadie whispered, reaching in for the door handle. "Everything's gonna be—"

She touched the handle and jerked back, barely containing a shriek as pain seared her hand. She held it up. Her palm was bright pink, her fingers still sizzling.

"Silver shitting son of a *bitch*," Sadie hissed nonsensically. She sucked on her burned fingers, her cool tongue soothing the burn.

Take two. She reached in with her other hand, bracing herself before wrenching the handle as fast as she could.

Her fingers flashed with heat. The car door creaked open. Sadie kicked it the rest of the way and leaned in, pulling at Clarissa's bonds with crispy fingers.

Clarissa clambered onto the grass with shaky legs.

"Oh my god, *thank* you, that was so scary. He kept telling me to stop crying, like, what do you WANT me to do, jerk!" Clarissa sniffed, looking wildly around the field of parked cars. "Where's Honey?"

Sadie pointed behind them at Sapphire Palace. "Distracting him."

"What? Oh my god, go *get* her!"

"I'm gonna," Sadie said, gripping her shaking shoulders. "But first we need to make sure he never does this shit to anyone else ever again."

"Like..." Clarissa trailed off. She took a breath, as if

about to ask a question. Then she paused, her expression flickering with decision. Whatever she had been going to ask, she didn't want to know the answer.

"Okay," she said instead, voice wavering. "What do we do?"


Sadie led her into Sapphire Palace, Clarissa clutching a rope from Elijah's car behind her back. They lingered near the doors, watching Honey get ready to climb onto stage. The ceiling dimmed, the stage lights growing brighter.

"Where is he?" Clarissa whispered.

Sadie scanned the crowd. Elijah lurked in the middle, a few people shooting strange looks at the leather-jacket wearing, toothpick-chewing stranger. His hand was in his coat, glowering up at Honey as she stalked onto stage.

"He won't shoot me," Clarissa whispered, her eyes wide and trusting. "Right?"

"Of course not," Sadie said, hoping it wasn't a lie. "Ready?"

Clarissa jerked her head in a fearful nod.

"Good," Sadie told her, and ran for the stage.

Honey adjusted the microphone. Feedback screeched over the crowd, and Sadie fought the urge to screech in pain as she clambered onto the stage. Vampire hearing sucked sometimes.

Sadie slunk behind Honey, grabbing her guitar. Honey didn't look at her.

"Sorry about that," said Honey in a decent approximation of Marilyn Munroe's breathy tone. Then she giggled, all Honey. "I'm just joking, no way I'm keeping that up all night. How's everybody doing?"

A whoop went up from the crowd. Too many people had their phones out, cameras aimed at the stage. Some of them were tracking Sadie as she crossed the stage and picked up her guitar, their nervous grins lit up by their phone screens. Even Britney and Summer had their phones out—Summer pretending she was checking her reflection, Britney struggling to take photos with a hand half-covered in a cast.

And in the middle of it all: Elijah, chewing his toothpick hard. His hand shifted under his coat. Sadie tried not to picture Elijah's scarred fingers clutching a silver crossbow beneath the leather.

She glanced at the double doors. Clarissa had dragged the first one shut.

"Well," Honey continued, swiveling her hips. "Your night's about to get even better. Where's our birthday boy?"

Another whoop. Ken Lu raised his hand, looking bashful. It didn't suit him.

Honey blew him a kiss. "This one's for you."

Sadie started strumming, ignoring the pain in her singed fingers. *Happy Birthday,* nice and slow. The very first thing she learned to play after her parents got her a guitar for her sixth birthday. Coincidentally, also the day Honey decided they were going to be in a band together.

Honey's red lips curved into a smirk. No one could tell she was terrified. No one except Sadie, lurking in the shadows behind her, acting like she'd never kissed that cold mouth.

Elijah glared up at them, his face twisted in disgust.

Sadie glanced at the double door. Clarissa had dragged the second one shut, fumbling with the ropes. Her grip skidded and slipped as she tried to make a knot.

Elijah turned his head, following Sadie's gaze.

Honey sucked in a breath, leaning into the microphone.

*Please*, Sadie prayed, watching Elijah's eyes widen on Clarissa. *Please...*

"Happy birthday," Honey crooned. "Mr. Ken-i-dent—"

Elijah yelled, hauling his crossbow out of his coat.

Sadie's fingers dug into the chords, stopping the music. Sapphire Palace fell into shocked silence. Ken stood on his tiptoes to search for his mother, who had certainly not approved *this* last-minute change.

"Excuse *you*," Honey said. She fluttered her eyelashes, a flash of Marilyn Munroe grace or a hint of nervousness at the crossbow aiming at her heart. "Save all your cheering for the—"

Elijah squeezed the trigger.

Sadie forced herself not to blur into action, her cold heart twisting in her chest as the arrow sailed over the crowd.

Honey shrieked, ducking to the side. The arrow

embedded in the wall behind the stage, but not before it exploded through a flower dangling from the ceiling. Plastic petals rained down over the stage, a shard of white skimming Sadie's cheek.

Elijah turned to face the screaming crowd, crossbow aloft.

"They're locking you in," he bellowed, spitting the toothpick out and reloading his crossbow. "I'm trying to save you, you idiots!"

By the door, Clarissa yanked the ropes away from the handles and scurried around the back of the crowd, dumping the ropes as she went. Towards the knot on the other side of the room that held the giant *18* aloft.

Honey sobbed. No tears, obviously. But it was impressive how convincing she could be, even with her face dry.

"Oh my *god*," she yelled. "He's crazy, *please* help me, he's been stalking me."

Sadie cleared her throat and spoke loudly enough for the retreating first row to hear: "You too?"

They'd agreed on this in the narrow hallway outside the bathrooms. It made it sound like they didn't hang out. That they were innocent bystanders caught up in something that had nothing to do with them.

Honey turned to look at her, all dread and surprise. If Sadie was watching from below, she might have believed they were two bewildered strangers who once loved each other beyond recognition.

"Hey!" Ken called, forcing himself through his scared

classmates toward Elijah. "Who the hell do you think you are, man?"

He twisted to hiss at his mom through the crowd— "Call the cops, holy shit!"—and then confronted Elijah, hands up, panting. Like he could take on a guy with a crossbow with nothing but big hair and entitlement.

"It's not REAL, you crazy shit," he spat. "Honey wasn't even in the same *state* when those guys got killed. You believe everything you see online, man?"

"You think you know," Elijah said darkly. "You think you *know*."

At the far wall, Clarissa perched next to the rope. She was holding a bowie knife, also stolen from Elijah's truck. She rested the blade over the thick rope, ready to slice. She stared at Sadie, waiting.

"We were just bored," Ken tried, looking to his classmates for support. "Right? Guys? Nothing to do in this town, so when we saw that video we took it and ran."

He stood on his tiptoes, looking over the sea of heads. "Brit? Where's Brit?"

Britney gasped. She was at the edge of the crowd, slowly edging toward the door. She held her injured arm close to her chest, a frightened smile frozen on her face, jaw working as she chewed her cherry gum in overtime.

"It's totally fake," she blurted. "I...I just wanted something to talk about."

"See?" Ken pointed at the girls on stage, Honey cowering in her Marilyn dress, Sadie wrestling her guitar strap off. "Just a couple of teenage girls! No vampires here!"

"They're going—" Elijah stopped, jaw tensing as he saw the doors: still closed, but no ropes tying them shut. "You don't know what they are. The hunger—it's relentless. Nothing can stop it."

Sadie's stomach howled. All that animal blood and it wasn't sated. Honey had to cave her head in to make her let go of Mr. Lu. Maybe...

"I'll show you," Elijah snarled. He grabbed Ken's arm, shoving up his pristine sleeve to expose his wrist.

"What are you doing?" Ken barked, fear bleeding into his voice. He looked around desperately. "Mom?"

"The police are on their way," called Ken's mom through the crowd, her hand trembling around the phone at her ear.

Elijah ignored them, pulling an arrow from his jacket.

Honey's eyes widened. She turned to Sadie once more, her mouth moving around words so quiet only Sadie could hear.

*"Just keep looking at me."*

The arrow glinted in the dim lights.

"Don't," Ken yelped, but it was too late. Elijah brought the arrow down, slashing the tip across Ken's wrist.

Ken howled, almost loud enough to drown out his mom's scream. Blood poured onto the polished floorboards.

"SHOW THEM WHAT YOU ARE," Elijah bellowed. It was loud, the loudest thing in the room, even with all the panicked screams. But it paled in comparison to Ken's heartbeat, a siren song dragging Sadie in.

The screams fell away. The room fell away. Her classmates fell away. Honey, resplendent and infuriating and scared and beautiful—fell away. The world narrowed into blood dripping down that warm wrist.

Then, just as she felt her eyes flickering black, the world expanded again. Honey stepped in front of her, hands on Sadie's elbows, face drawn and determined. She'd covered up her freckles with makeup, but Sadie could still see them. Sadie had kissed every single of them.

"What'd I say?" Honey asked her. "I said look! At! Me! You're not looking, and I'm *so* hot right now."

Her voice was lost in that throbbing heartbeat. Sadie squeezed her eyes shut, the black flickering in and out of them. She glanced over to the wall where Clarissa was waiting, her hand trembling around the knife.

Honey's mouth grazed her ear. Sadie could already hear her coming up with excuses: *it was crazy up there, I was just comforting her, old habits die hard.*

"You're bigger than this," Honey whispered. "You're nothing compared to this. Hear me? This hunger isn't shit. You look at me, alright? Stay here. Be here."

"'M looking," Sadie mumbled. The black leached out of her eyes. She gripped Honey's elbows, looking into that lovely face she'd known since first grade.

"I'm always looking," Sadie whispered.

So quiet. Nobody else would've heard it among all the screaming. But Honey did.

Sadie gave her a nod. Honey barely had time to frown, confused, before Sadie ripped out of her grip, climbed down off the stage, and stalked toward Elijah. Everyone in front of him had cleared out, running for the door, teenagers streaming out into the night. Only Ken's mom remained, screaming for her husband as she tried to tug her son free.

Elijah's arm was a brace across Ken's chest, holding him still, a crossbow pointed at his throat.

"What the hell," Ken chanted, clawing desperately at Elijah's arm. "What the hell, what the *hell*. Mom, ow, that *hurts*—"

His mom yanked harder on his elbow.

Elijah bared his blunt teeth. "You hungry bitch," he spat at Sadie. "You destroy everything. You just wait."

"Get away from us, weirdo," Sadie screamed, and charged.

Human speed. Too slow. Elijah bellowed again, throwing Ken to the side. Ken stumbled into his mother's waiting arms with a wheezed, "This birthday *sucks*."

Blood flowed down his arm. Sadie ignored it, forcing her legs to stay their course as she slammed into Elijah and shoved his crossbow up, the arrow aimed straight above them—at lightbulbs and flowers, not the hanging *18*. Not yet. That was a few steps behind them.

Elijah huffed, his finger flinching on the trigger. An

arrow slammed into the ceiling, raining white plastic petals and thin glass down on their heads.

"What?" he said with gritted teeth, his face twisting in confusion. "Not good enough for your vampire strength? Maybe I should've slit that kid's throat, *then* you would've—"

Sadie shoved him, letting through a little of her true strength. She felt like was riding the edge of human and vampire, eyes flickering again, the scent of blood thick in her nose.

Elijah grunted, stumbling back. Right underneath the wooden *18*.

"Right," he said, loading another arrow. He hauled the crossbow back up, a bolt of silver aimed right at Sadie's heart.

Sadie looked over. Clarissa's knife broke through the rope. There was a loud *snap*. Elijah's head whipped up, his rugged face transforming with terror as he watched the installation drop toward him.

Sadie closed her eyes. It didn't matter. She smelled every drop of blood that burst out of him when the wood hit him. She heard every bone that cracked and every inch of his agonized cry.

When she opened her eyes, they were flickering black and Honey was next to her. Other than a shaky Clarissa and a dying Elijah, Sapphire Palace was empty. The doors hung open, the sound of chatter and yells in the distance. Cars peeled out of the grassy parking lot.

Clarissa sniffled, hugging her elbows. "What now?"

Honey looked down at Elijah, considering. The *18* had crushed his lower torso and legs. He glared up at them hatefully, twitching with convulsions. His mouth fell open.

"There's...more of us," he croaked, blood dribbling down his chin. "You...can't...escape..."

"Would you shut *up*," Honey told him. She brought up the flat of her high heel and slammed it across Elijah's head. His neck snapped sideways, one last horrible breath bubbling out of him before his eyes went flat and lifeless.

Honey shuddered. "Okay. Let's go."

Sadie nodded. It was hard to move, every part of her screaming to bend down and suck the still-warm blood from Elijah's body.

Honey took her hand. Her palm was cold, a soothing balm for the burns.

"Hey," she said. "You with me?"

Sadie swallowed. Her singed fingers twitched against Honey's, the heat already leaching out.

"I'm here, babe," she croaked. "I'm with you."

Honey smiled. Not her knowing smirk or the grin she'd flashed at the crowd. But a tiny, private smile Sadie had treasured since she was small.

chapter
## **sixteen**

TWO WEEKS LATER, Honey ran into Mr. Lu walking his dog past the playground.

She waved from the swing. The one next to her was empty, swaying gently despite the lack of wind.

Mr. Lu squinted through the bright evening light, gripping Buster's leash as he started to growl.

"Stop it," he told the dog. "Honey, hello. How have you been?"

Honey smiled impishly. With bright red lipstick and a pink hoodie studded with hearts, she was the only spot of color on the ruined playground.

"Oh, you know me," she said, shaking her hair so it glowed in the sunset. "The fun times never stop. How about you? No more bandage chic?"

Mr. Lu raised his free hand to touch his forehead, where a shiny red line sat just below his hairline. No white gauze peeked out from his tidy shirt collar. He still stunk of sweat, but Honey was mostly sure that was nerves.

"No more bandage chic," he said, saying the last word like he wasn't entirely sure of the pronunciation.

"Love it," Honey said. "And the fam?"

"Ken's doing fine," Mr. Lu said with a thin smile. "I'm sure Summer and Britney keep you updated."

"Britney and I don't talk much anymore," Honey said. "But Summer's a great little news gal."

Ken had taken a week off school after his disastrous birthday party, which ended with a dead stranger embedded in the floorboards, five stitches in Ken's arm, and thousands of dollars' worth of damages they only got out of because the Lu family threatened to sue.

When Ken did show up at school, his arm was still swathed in bandages and he yelled at anyone who tried to bring up his birthday, even if it was to congratulate him for trying to talk Elijah down. He even yelled when he overheard someone bringing it up to Sadie in the cafeteria, which had been so surprising the whole room had gone silent.

*What?* he'd snapped as everyone stared. *Think it's funny some weirdo tried to kill them? It's not! Everyone go back to your juice boxes!*

Then he'd gone back to his food, picking at his bandage and not looking at anybody. Not even Britney, who had taken to sitting at his table during lunch.

Summer said Britney felt guilty about posting the YouTube comment that led Elijah to the party. It was probably true. She didn't even make Sadie's life hell for spraining her wrist, which was as close to apologizing as Britney would ever get.

Buster barked. Mr. Lu tugged on his leash.

"Hey," he said. "Calm down."

Honey watched the dog tremble. She'd killed animals much larger than him. She wondered if he could sense it.

Mr. Lu cleared his throat. He reached under his shirt collar, scratching gingerly at his wound. "Are you and Sadie Greer spending time together nowadays? Summer said she saw you hugging on stage when that man—"

Honey cut him off. "When that guy tried to shoot us with a *crossbow*? Yeah, we freaked out a little."

"Sorry. I didn't mean—"

"No, it's fine." Honey rubbed the rusty swing chain, grimacing when rust flecked off on her finger. "Weird stuff happens when you think you're going to die, I guess. Me and Sadie Greer are ancient history, Mr. Lu. Nothing to dig up. We're...*very* different people."

Mr. Lu nodded, staring down at the rotting playground bark. He never was good at meeting people's gazes when he was uncomfortable. Like father, like son. Ken hadn't looked Honey in the eyes since he ran out of the Sapphire Palace with a bleeding arm.

Buster barked.

Honey blew him a kiss.

Buster barked louder, straining his leash back toward the path. Trying to get away.

"Well," Mr. Lu said. "I better leave before it gets

dark."

"Don't run into any bears," Honey told him.

Mr. Lu blinked. His hand twitched upward, like he was going to reach under his shirt collar again. Then his hand dropped. He gave Honey a strange, stiff smile.

"I'll do my best," he said, and set off.

Honey waited until he was out of earshot. Then she sighed.

"Okay," she said. "He's gone."

Sadie emerged from the holey slide before Honey could finish talking, picking moss from her hair. The sunset behind her made her look like a strange summer spirit in cozy flannel.

"Better than gum," Honey called.

Sadie rolled her eyes and dropped into the swing next to her. "He totally suspects."

"So? What's he gonna do?" Honey swung sideways, the chains creaking dangerously as their hips bumped. "Anything fun happen in there?"

"Yeah, actually." Sadie dug out her phone. "Clarissa put up a new video."

Honey pushed down the knee-jerk panic. Clarissa had taken down any videos related to The Bleeding Bastards murders and promised not to film any more. Her subscriber count had suffered for it, but she assured them it was a worthwhile price to make sure Honey and Sadie didn't get tracked down again. Even if she did have to go back and work for that hot dog hut to pay rent to her parents.

Sadie pulled up the video. Honey leaned over to watch. The video was paused at twenty-nine seconds, Clarissa in mid-word in front of a wall in her childhood bedroom. The butterfly clip was back, but the drawn-on hearts were gone from her cheeks.

"Nobody's seen the bassist since the murders," Clarissa said. "The last they saw was him fleeing the building, splattered with blood. *Pretty* sus, if you ask me. Anyway, that's all I'm going to say about it. Now, onto today's topic: Mothman. Is he moth-man or moth-myth?"

Sadie paused the video and put her phone away. "She's been deleting any comments that have to do with us or The Bleeding Bastards murders. But she says they've been mostly sympathetic. Since word got out that some crazy guy tried to kill us, we've gone from suspects to two teenage girls caught up in an internet conspiracy."

Honey hummed, leaning over to rest her chin on Sadie's shoulder. "She's still got an eye out for our sire, right?"

"Patrolling all the Reddit boards," Sadie confirmed. "And...I don't know, she talks like she has *connections* now. Like, more than us and Milly's people."

Honey hummed again, digging her chin hard into Sadie's shoulder.

"Ow," said Sadie uselessly. As if a chin-dig could actually hurt her now. Honey could dig her fingernails in and it would take a decent amount of vampire strength for her to even feel it.

Sadie pulled back, giving Honey a questioning look. "What is it?"

Honey shrugged. She plucked at the sleeve of her hoodie, pulling a shred of pink from the center of a heart.

"We could try hanging out," she suggested, fiddling with the string. "Like, where people can see us. I really want to see everyone's faces after we make out in front of them."

Sadie gave her the look of someone long-suffering and charmed. "Okay, I'm not making out with you in front of *anyone*. You think I'm a PDA girl? 'Cause I'm not."

Honey ducked in, pressing a kiss to her neck. Sadie shoved her away, giggling in a way Honey hadn't heard in weeks.

"It's safer this way," Sadie protested. "Elijah—he said there were more. *Milly* says there are more. We don't want any more whispers. Besides, it's just for the rest of the year. Then we're outta here."

Honey dropped the string and linked their pinkies together. "I'll go to college."

"And major in bugs."

"And major in bugs," Honey agreed, not bothering with yet another lengthy explanation of all the specializations her degree could branch off into. She saved that for occasions when she wanted Sadie to look at her like she was trying desperately to look bored, all the while hiding her charmed smile.

Honey continued, "You tag along and find a community college or some cafe with cool coworkers who let you skim from the cash register. Your hunger *will* chill the hell out, like it's supposed to."

"And we'll find your sire and turn you human."

"We'll find a way to turn us *both* human," Honey corrected.

Sadie didn't answer. Her pinkie tightened around Honey's, hanging in the air between them.

Honey pressed her face into Sadie's neck. It felt like the kind of moment to say something big, something true, but she didn't want to ruin it.

"You should teach me how to drive," she said instead.

Sadie's laugh was so loud it made birds take off from the trees. Honey didn't turn to watch. She was too busy admiring her girlfriend's pale face lighting up with joy, head thrown back with it.

"You are not laying one dead finger on Steve-van's steering wheel."

Honey snickered into her neck. "I'll talk you into it. You *loooove* me."

"Ugh," Sadie said. "I know."

She squeezed Honey's pinkie. Honey squeezed back.

They stayed there, swinging gently, long after the sun went down. Sometimes talking, sometimes just looking. Seeing each other perfectly through the dark.


END.

# thank you

Thank you so much for reading Honeybites!

If you want to support me, please leave a review on Goodreads, Amazon or any social media of your choice.

Sign up to my newsletter at isbelleauthor.com for exciting updates and the first book in my spooky sapphic YA romance series, BABYLOVE!

# acknowledgments

A big thanks to Chloe Spencer, my beta reader and American consultant. Thank you for putting up with yet more messages sent at 3am PST such as WALK ME THROUGH HOW AN AMERICAN MAKES COFFEE AT HOME and DO YOU GUYS HAVE FREE PERIODS? Truly a legend.

Thank you to my cover artist Sophie Zuckerman (@dextrose.png on Insta!) for another baller cover.

Thank you to my wonderful formatter, Edward Giordano, and Catriona Turner, my editor. You're consistently amazing, and I'd be lost without you.

# about the author

I. S. Belle writes LGBT Romance, Paranormal and Horror Young Adult books. She works in a bookstore in New Zealand and stops to pat dogs in the street. If you have a dog and your local bookshop allows pets - for the love of booksellers, please bring them in.

She has a Creative Writing Masters from the International Institute of Modern Letters. You can find her on Tiktok @i.s.belle_writes or on Instagram @isbelleauthor.

also by i. s. belle

**BABYLOVE SERIES**

BABYLOVE

SUGARSNAP

SWEETHEARTS

**ZOMBABE**

ZOMBABE

**HONEYBLOODS SERIES**

HONEYBLOODS

HONEYBITES

**GIRLS NIGHT**

GIRLS NIGHT